MW01047274

LOSHI

and the

BATTLE

for the

GOD STONES

BY
THEO KOUTALOS

Copyright 2021

All rights reserved. This book or any portion thereof may not be reproduced or
used in any manner whatsoever without the express written permission of the
publisher except for the use of brief quotations in a book review.

ISBN: 978-1-66781-157-4 (print)
ISBN: 978-1-66781-158-1 (eBook)

PROLOGUE

Once upon a time, before beasts and humans walked the earth, insects of all sizes reigned over all the land and forests. Each of its kind had an empire and a ruler, enslaving the weak and feeble. As time progressed, so too did each ruler's ambitions for power over the forests and all the other empires within them. War fell upon the trees like a raging storm as insects battled each other in the relentless pursuit of domination over the lands.

In the end, a thousand battles and a million deaths resulted in mass extinctions of insect species; those who survived were again, left to somehow rebuild what was left.

But out of the ashes rose a new beginning for those who made it through this devastation. An era of Kings and Queens was born, and territories were formed for all who dwelled within them to prosper and thrive. Order was seemingly restored in the forests, and life continued on.

Meanwhile, deep inside the vast woodlands of Orayu, was a mighty empire called the Adephaga. The Adephaga was truly majestic in size and dominion, and lived within an enormous dead sequoia trunk that had been destroyed many moons prior. On the outside, the tree trunk seemed lifeless; on the inside, however, it was alive and home to a vast number of black beetles.

The black beetles who lived in the Adephaga were not like ordinary beetles. Likewise, this tree trunk was no ordinary piece of dead wood. The oral traditions state that one night, the universe had sprinkled the earth with its origins. As millions of stars blanketed the sphere like raindrops, a falling star hit this tree, leaving a magnificent green stone in its heart. The stone emanated a glow so marvelous, it was impossible to not be drawn to it.

The tree came alive as its leaves changed shape and its budded flowers opened and flared with brilliant color. For many years, the black beetles laid their eggs in the opening as the glowing green stone warmed the growing embryos. The mysterious power of this stone made the beetles different in many wondrous ways. They possessed great strength, superior intellect, and their capabilities were unsurpassed by any other of their kind. For this reason, the Adephaga was unique in its supremacy. For generations they continued to evolve into an advanced species of beetle, changing the future of their kind for generations.

One night, a ferocious storm ripped through the forest and lightning struck the tree breaking it in half. The giant tree crashed down breaking the stone into three pieces. Two stones were lost in the tempest, but one was miraculously retrieved by the beetles. They frantically sought the two missing stones for years and years, but they were never found. Despite this, even as a third of its entirety, the remaining stone's power was tremendous in strength. It enchanted whomever touched it; one could only imagine the possibilities for the insect that could unite the three pieces, as it would amplify the true nature of whomever carried the stone.

And so this was to be, the quest for all insects, from kingdom to kingdom. A true test from the Gods, in the age of the God Stones.

Part 1

Tangled Webs are Woven

The Black Beetles of the Adephaga were highly intelligent. They built a metropolis in the sky, and demonstrated a unique mastering of architectural design on the ground. Their homes were built into the inner tree walls with hundreds of dwellings with staircases that zigged, zagged, swerved and swirled. Schools, businesses, and recreational facilities were also constructed off-ground to further farming opportunities for an innovative agricultural wonder that provided for all in the community. A true sustainable wonder for all to live in and benefit from.

During the day, the Adephaga was abuzz with activity. On a breezy day, the air would be filled with delicious aromas from beetles cooking and baking. If one breathed in deep enough, one could almost taste the hearty and familiar foods as they cooked and cooled. After dark, all was quiet and peaceful. The night sky would light up with millions of stars, and once in awhile, the brilliant silvery moon would reveal itself.

The beetles lived happily and harmoniously in the Adephaga. It was a well-functioning monarchy that governed its citizens in a fair and peaceful manner. They were ruled by King Tearon, his Queen, Elytra, and their beautiful daughter, Princess Loshi. They were adored by all, and this adoration was reciprocated as well. The King truly loved the beetles in his kingdom, and it was evident in his actions as a ruler.

King Tearon was a good and benevolent King, but as is so common with any ruler, his family's past was not without a history of tyranny and war.

Tearon was the son of the mighty Dynastis, a slave warrior turned King. He had overthrown the ruthless Ediuss, a ferocious Warlord who had once enslaved all black beetles under his reign. Ediuss was the carrier of two stones, using it's extraordinary power for his triumph of terror.

Legend has it that Dynastis, who was born a slave, was gripped with rage after the death of his wife, Sarha, at the hands of Ediuss' guards. Sarha was noticeably beautiful and Ediuss' reign of power gave those of rank rule over whom they wished, at times with salacious savagery. Dynastis was bloodthirsty and swore brutal retribution against the barbaric dictator. This bitter rage festered in him day and night, this unjust act of cruelty playing over in his mind endlessly.

On the fateful night of reckoning, determined to avenge his beloved, Dynastis left his only child Tearon with a trusted female beetle to care for him and slipped off into the night. Upon reaching the palace walls undetected, he made his way carefully across the main bridge leading through the tall gates. Undeterred by what awaited him, he scurried quietly through the dark corridors, slaying the unsuspecting soldiers in his path as others in the palace slept soundly in their beds.

He moved between the shadows, quiet as the night sky surrounding the palace, and crept into Ediuss' bedchamber, across the floor, to his bedside.

But Ediuss was not there.

Instead, Ediuss' wife slept alone in their bed - peaceful, unsuspecting, defenseless. Dynastis approached her bedside and placed his dagger to her throat - one swift motion, and he could inflict the same pain upon Ediuss as was inflicted upon him. It would be over.

But as he gripped the handle tighter and leaned in, he heard a tiny sound and carefully pulled the sheet down, revealing an infant in her arms. The baby smiled up at him and playfully giggled, reaching its tiny hand up to him and squeezing his finger.

Suddenly, as if sensing Dynastis' presence, Ediuss' wife stirred and awoke. Before her eyes could adjust to what was lurking in the dim lighting, he had already vanished.

Feeling unsettled, she slowly opened the door and peered into the hallway, only to see several beetle guards lying dead on the ground. She stifled a scream and retreated to her bed, gripping her crying child to her chest tightly.

In the chaos, she noticed something in her periphery outside her window. She slowly rose back to her feet, walked closer to the aperture, and saw Dynastis fleeing into the forest.

She sighed a sigh of dread as he disappeared from view.

* * *

Alarm horns bellowed throughout the land as search parties scoured the forest to find the intruder. Dynastis changing course, unavoidably stumbling through the dangerous forests of Arathma, the spider forests. He ventured carefully through its nexus, navigating the weblike terrain, swatting away at the nebulous cloud of floating particles that surrounded him. Ahead in the gloomy distance, the outline of the Cave of the Dead emerged, a dark and tenebrous spider sanctuary where no insect ever dared to enter. Its appearance was far more haunting than it was welcoming, but Dynastis was exhausted and in need of somewhere to rest until morning.

Oblivious to the dangerous creature that was watching him, he approached the mouth of the cave, peering in carefully.

A fearsome voice echoed throughout the hollow.

"Who dares to enter here?"

Dynastis crept in fearfully as the voice reverberated through the moist capacious walls. Nervously, he answered "I didn't mean to disturb you, I am a slave looking for refuge and rest. When I am strong, I will leave, for I seek revenge on my devils."

A giant black and white striped spider moved into the path of a beam of moonlight, revealing his downtrodden and battered body. He looked at Dynastis with distaste and replied, "I also seek revenge. Your kind has taken everything from me, everything! They came like a plague and left with that which had once made us Gods."

Dynastis' eyes darted around the dark lair. They adjusted to the moonlight that shone through holes in the cavernous walls, and fell upon the faint silhouettes of dead spiders scattered around the rocky mounds. He realized he had come face to face with Bolas, the elder spider Lord.

Dynastis had heard Bolas' name in stories as a child, but never imagined he would have stumbled upon him in this way. Dynastis inched closer to the imposing spider, only to notice that he was caressing two small infant spiders laying dead at his side. Their bodies were decomposed and frail, the stench of death emanated from them and filled Dynastis' senses. Bolas wept softly as he looked despairingly upon the lifeless corpses.

Suddenly, his sobs turned to heavy, shuddering breaths. His gaze of sadness turned to glowering rage. The legs of his children rattled as he began to snap and break their bodies in trembling anger. The giant spider suddenly lurched towards Dynastis, who flinched, but Bolas collapsed in pain halfway.

Seeing the mighty Bolas as a now decrepit arachnid evoked pity in Dynastis, and he again moved closer to him, "I am not your enemy, old spider; I am not here to burden you. All I seek is vengeance."

Bolas stared vacantly into Dynastis' eyes, as if wanting to be put out of his misery.

"Your wretched leader Ediuss took the stone that gave birth to our strength. The stone that changed our destiny. Now he carries two stones, and his power is a danger like nothing ever seen before."

Dynastis pressed further.

"I know your pain, Lord Bolas. Ediuss took my beloved from me, the mother of my child. His malice knows no bounds. He must be stopped, or all will be lost."

A brief glimmer of hope flickered over Bolas' face as Dynastis reached out to help the old spider to his legs. Bolas accepted and was lifted up off the ground. As a result of this encounter, a covenant was made between Dynastis and the Spider God Bolas that together, they would destroy Ediuss and his army, regain the stones, and restore their species' legacies.

On that day, an allegiance was born of beetle and spider; they built an army of strength and size like no other. They plotted and strategized over time, and on the day of the full moon, they descended upon Ediuss' palace. In a storm of viciousness, they fought to overthrow the leader and his henchmen. It was a bloody battle, but in the end, Ediuss and his soldiers were decimated. Dynastis and Bolas reclaimed their stones and set about working to restore order and equilibrium to their respective species.

For a time, there was peace. No insect could have predicted what would happen next.

* * *

Having been reunited with the stones, Bolas became enamored with their power. His wonder and awe was all-consuming. He began demanding that he hold both stones in his custody, instead of sharing the stones between the two leaders as previously agreed.

When Dynastis refused Bolas and challenged his obsession with the stones, Bolas became hostile. Dynastis demanded that Bolas surrender his stone once he realized that he was no longer trustworthy. Bolas became incensed. Breaking their pact, he ordered his spider troops to attack Dynastis and his beetle army, resulting in yet another bloody battle.

The massacre ended with Dynastis and Bolas left to fight to the death. Bolas was all powerful and with smugness he did not use the rings power in a show of strength. Mistakingly, he was no match for Dynastis' strength and skill, but as Dynastis had seemingly overpowered the treasonous spider lord, Bolas delivered a final venomous strike to the chest.

As Dynastis lay dying on the blood-soaked ground, he managed to roll to his side, observing the carnage on the land around him. Without a sound or a breath in the air, he painfully crawled to the body of Bolas. He rested his forehead on his blood-soaked furry chest and plunged his dagger into his side. The spider lord's body lurched, and then was lifeless.

As Dynastis slid himself off Bolas' body, he noticed a green light shining through his armor. Dynastis tore it open to reveal the ring hanging upon a root-woven neckless around Ediuss' neck. Dynastis slowly brought the two stones together in a wondrous array of light. The two jagged green stones fused together, bursting bright in magnificence. Its mysterious power and brilliance shone against the bleakness of the battlefield.

Dynastis grasped the ring and held it tightly as the green light slowly moved up his arm, eventually engulfing him completely. He was bewildered at the stones' enchantment, consuming him and healing him with every breathe. The wound on his chest was inevitably life ending yet, it gave him enough strength to rise off the ground. He curiously slipped on the ring and to his amazement, a glowing chrome green sword began to take shape in his hand, designed to perfection and stronger than any metal he had ever felt. He knew then that something incredible, inexplicable, was happening and it was all because of this stone.

The ground began to rumble and shake - the wind became violent, whipping ashes and debris all around Dynastis. He felt somehow lifted, despite his battered state. But before he could understand what was happening to him, he felt a searing pain shoot through his arm. He looked down and to his horror, saw that an arrow had pierced his hand, severing half of it. The ring fell to the ground, splitting the stones in two again.

Dynastis, confused at what had just happened and unable to see, frantically felt the ground around him with his other hand. Feeling the hard smooth surface of one of the stones, he snatched it up and quickly stuffed it safely under his wing.

All the sudden, Dynastis heard the pounding of feet approaching him. He squinted his large black eyes into the dusty darkness, but couldn't make out where it was coming from. He heard the footsteps coming closer and closer until he felt something knock him swiftly down, hitting the ground hard with a thud.

Dynastis felt the weight of something press his head into the cold earth.

Unable to make out his attacker and struggling to breathe, out of the corner of his eye Dynastis was able to see a faint reddish glow on the ground. The second stone faintly appeared. Almost as quickly as he saw it and was snatched up before he could even budge.

Just then, he felt the warm breath of the unknown creature on his neck.

"Zoondaaaaa..."

Before the sound had even left Dynastis' ear, the creature disappeared into the black abyss.

All became quiet. The wind calmed and the dust settled as the faint sound of the second infantry of soldiers approached.

Dynastis' battered body, weak from battle and from the venomous sting of Bolas, lay motionless on the ground. His breathing was labored, his facade expressionless.

From behind a pile of rubble, a beetle soldier appeared. Then two, five, six more. A steady stream of beetles began to emerge from the soot and approached their brave and weary leader. They turned him over as blood bubbled out of his chest and mouth; his breath was growing more and more shallow by the second.

Seeing that the fate of Dynastis was inevitable, and fighting back emotion, one beetle shouted "All hail our brave King, Dynastis!"

As if on cue, the entire crowd of beetles dropped to one knee and echoed "All hail our brave King, Dynastis!"

The dying King clutched the lone glowing stone to his chest as two beetles held him in their arms. Feeling the warmth of his comrades, but knowing he was slipping away, Dynastis spoke out one final command through gritted teeth.

"From this day forward, all beetles are free. My son will carry on my reign, and there will be peace. The stone shall be used for good, not for bloodshed."

As Dynastis gasped his final breath, the stone flickered and went out.

Dynastis was given all the burial rites of a ruler. His young son Tearon was crowned King of all black beetles that lived within the Adephaga.

And so it was to be, King Tearon continued his father's legacy of peace and order in the Adephaga, with the sacred stone once held by his father now adorning his hand. Unaware of its true power, and its role in the fate that lay ahead for him.

Part 2

The Pinnacle to the Pit

Safety and stability was of utmost importance to King Tearon, and were vital to the royal family's existence. The exterior palace walls were constructed out of an assortment of nut shells and honey mortar, which created an impenetrable shield against dangerous insect predators.

The territory was also secured and protected by the King's trusted defense minister, General Hillius, a long-horned beetle who was highly skilled in the ancient methods of combat. Under his command, the Adephaga were protected by a militia of highly skilled Shadow Beetles, as the citizens slept soundly through the night. The militia were as invisible as ghosts, and deadly as any predator in the forest.

Each soldier was unnamed, never having revealed their true identities to anyone, not even their own families. They left home under cover of darkness, never indicating to their loved ones where they were going or the purpose of their flight. Once making the commitment to be a soldier in the Shadow Beetle army, they surrendered ego and individuality in order to serve the commonwealth and maintain a unified front.

As Loshi grew in age, so too did she grow in beauty - so much so that word of her grace and allure spread throughout the land, resulting in King Tearon's fierce protectiveness of his beloved daughter.

Loshi's tenacity began to take shape as she became both curious and restless; her desire to see beyond the Adephaga was rapidly developing, as she found life as a Princess to be dull and unexciting. She began to feel envious of other beetles her age. She longingly gazed out her bedchamber window at them walking to school each day, laughing and mucking about, teasing each other and chattering away.

King Tearon took notice, and saw this as a sign to be furtherly cautious of his daughter's enamoredness with the outside world. The way he saw it, she was far too valuable as a Princess and innocent as a daughter to be exposed to the volatility and unpredictability of the world outside their walls. He knew far too well about the dangers of that world, and vowed to protect his daughter at all costs from it.

Knowing this, the King decided it was necessary for Loshi to be home-schooled in the palace and enlisted General Hillius to personally train her in self-defense and archery every day. Loshi, while frustrated and feeling stifled by her father's strict ways of governing her growth, obeyed her father's wishes and flourished under her teacher and General Hillius' tutelage.

Hillius quickly noted how advanced Loshi was in comparison to his other students, but kept his admiration quiet. She was a swift learner, and demonstrated a capable mastery of the art of combat, which was passed on through generations of beetle soldiers. All this was extremely rare for a young beetle - a princess, no less. But Loshi never took her talents too seriously, instead coming off with an endearing naivete that somehow made her even more impressive and her strengths stand out even further.

Despite thriving in her studies and skills, every night as she drifted off to sleep, Loshi would stare out at the stars and imagine what life would be like if she was just a common beetle. No walls, rules, or fixed destinies. Some nights, she would get lost in these thoughts, looking off into the distance; picturing a life outside the kingdom, having adventures, and even falling in love.

Soon came the night before Loshi's traditional coming-of-age celebration. This event came only once in a lifetime for young members of royal families, and was a chance for eligible beetle bachelors to impress the King and Queen in hopes of earning their beloved daughter's hand in marriage.

Loshi was readying herself when some chatter in the courtyard below caught her ear. It was the King and Queen, unaware that their daughter could hear them. King Tearon sat in a chair as Queen Elytra gathered small bluebell flowers from the garden.

"I understand, but being a Princess means one day she will be a Queen, and therefore we will need to ensure she finds someone suitable. She is of age to marry, after all, and there just so happens to be an impressive young beetle, the son of a military family outside the Adephaga, who is seeking her hand. I am told that he is highly skilled in arithmetic, hunting and combat - he will arrive tomorrow to present himself."

The Queen interjected, "My King, no daughter of mine will have her husband snatched away by the hands of war. It's not the life that I want for her."

"Come now, my love, there hasn't been war for many moons!" The King laughed incredulously, before pausing and shaking his head. "If only Loshi were born a boy. It's so much easier with boys."

He paused and glanced down at his right hand, upon which the sacred green stone ring was placed. He took off his ring and handed it to Elytra. "Have them shine it, I want it to glisten like a star in the sky so that even the Gods are captivated by it."

As Elytra moved towards the castle, Tearon grabbed her wrist and pulled her in close.

"Just think...if she were to be married, we'd have the palace all to ourselves again."

Overhead, Loshi rolled her large black eyes and groaned at this display, not realizing how her nauseated sounds carried. The Queen glanced up at Loshi's bedroom - Loshi quickly moved away from the window and collapsed into her bed.

Just then, Loshi's handmaiden, a plump and pretty beetle named Aniya, skittered into the room and noticed Loshi appeared upset.

"Good evening Princess, are you not well?"

Loshi sat up with a sullen expression on her face, took a deep breath and shook her head.

"My father has succumbed to politics and has planned for me to meet my future prince."

"Oooh! Is he handsome?" Aniya gushed.

Loshi gave an exasperated sigh and flung herself back onto her bed, pulling the covers over her head. The maiden continued as she sat on the bed, "I bet he is devilishly handsome, like an aristabeetle...riding on pillbug back, with the sun beating on his strong black armor. His tentacles gleaming from the morning dew..."

Aniya stopped herself in embarrassment as Loshi stared back at her with confusion.

They both burst out laughing for a moment, before Loshi stopped herself.

"What if I don't love him? I cannot wed a beetle when I have nothing to compare him to! I have been a prisoner to these palace walls since the day I was born. I have never had any friends, have never explored the streets of my own city. No adventures, no first kiss. Now I will be forced to marry? Get fat, lay eggs, have a billion kids?"

As if on cue, the Queen cleared her throat to denote her presence in the doorway as she stepped in the room. "I hope I'm not interrupting."

Aniya clambered to her feet and lowered her head in reverence. "Of course not, my Queen - we were just talking about boys...I mean, b-books."

The Queen's smile vanished to a cold stare. Aniya's antennae twitched with embarrassment, and she ducked towards the doorway. "I will leave you both in peace."

Loshi looked at her mother and smirked slyly. "Don't you just love her?"

The Queen shook her head, stepped to the window and looked down with a smile. "Eavesdropping, my dear?" Loshi turned away.

The Queen walked over to the bed and sat. "Loshi, we have spoken many times about upholding traditions. It was the same for your father and I, and we grew to love each other very much." Loshi turned over, resting her head on her mother's lap and softly replied, "I always imagined things would be different. I suppose I was just being foolish."

The Queen nodded thoughtfully. "When I was your age, I imagined a different life for myself as well. But this life is the life that was meant for me to live, and I would never change anything because it has brought us you. As unreasonable as he may seem at times, you must know your father loves you."

Loshi wiped her tears away from her shiny black eyes. "What if I do not approve of this beetle?"

The Queen kissed Loshi's head and smiled.

"Have faith in your father; you know how overprotective he is. Now, get some rest...you will want to look your best tomorrow."

The Queen moved towards the bedchamber door and quietly closed it. Loshi stared into the night sky and caught a shooting star streak across the heavens. Feeling strangely reassured, she smiled and drifted off to sleep.

* * *

Tunneled deep beneath the roots and soils of the Adephaga, an evil was rising. An evil buried far beneath the peacefulness and beauty, an unknowing violence of imperial rule, unbeknownst to the Adephagans, and the royal family.

Nicro, The Dark Lord, stood in the darkness, only revealing his menacing silhouette as he watched his army of Death Beetles begin their preparation for war. The Death Beetles supervised thousands of enslaved ants as they hammered at glowing hot metal, almost in unison. Others smashed and chiseled at the muddy walls of the tunnels. The sounds of cracking whips and resulting screams begin to crossfade into the sound of rhythmic stomping of the D-Beetles squads marching in.

Nicro's loyal henchman, a thin, old and sickly looking beetle named Kring, sidled up to his master. "The hour is soon upon us, my Lord."

"Yes," Nicro growled. "You have outdone yourself Kring, and you will be rewarded once I am King."

Kring bowed to his Commander. "Your army is ready to kill, bleed, and die for you, my Lord. The weapon you desire is complete."

Kring motioned to two Death Beetles to unsheathe the massive war machine; a device so sinister in its creativity, so truly iniquitous.

The machine was made up of rows of caged venomous insects all being tortured to produce their poison, as it was sucked into an enormous glowing levitating sphere all blending together to create an ultimate killing concoction. In the centre of the sphere, a magnificent jagged green stone radiated, blending its power with the poisons. The deadly toxin was then poured into a blowing device that shot out delicate sacks onto a conveyor belt. The sacks were then sprayed, becoming hard as glass, and placed in metal claws that attached to the D-Beetles' armor.

Lord Nicro reached out his claw-like hand and retrieved one of the glass balls, raising it slowly over his head. The D-Beetles began to stomp their spears and swords menacingly in rhythm as Nicro gazed out over the sea of armored soldiers. The glow of the poison-filled glass ball illuminated his facade, revealing the chilling side profile of his mask.

"Tomorrow, we will crush every single beetle till all that's left is piles of twitching limbs! No more will we eat scraps; at dawn, we feast on Adephagan blood!"

The soldier beetles roared for their Leader. He stepped to the edge of a pit holding the poison packed ball above three tied-up ants trembling in fear.

"Long before beetles, ants ruled all kingdoms. They dominated without mercy. Now, look...we are more powerful than them!"

The three ants looked up in fear as they frantically pulled and tugged on the rope that was tying them to a leaf stem. The stem was suspended across the middle of the pit that was so deep, any sound made into it made no immediate echo. No insect had ever met the bottom of the pit and lived to tell about it. The petrified ants knew it was no use. This would not end well.

Suddenly, Nicro released the ball into the pit, and its glow vanished swiftly as it fell deeper and deeper into the black hole. All became eerily quiet, and the ants closed their eyes tightly, painfully bracing themselves for what awaited them.

The beetles and ants also braced until they heard the faint sound of glass breaking deep within the pit. Within seconds, the ants began to cough and choke violently as the poison rose quickly into the air and filled their tiny nostrils. Nicro looked on with great satisfaction as they shrieked and gasped for air, but it was all in vain.

Kring quietly observed Nicro's sadism out of the corner of his eye, and realized the depth of his Commander's wickedness. No one noticed as his smile slowly faded to fright.

Part 3

Celebration/Decimation

THOCK! The arrow struck the tree trunk just inches beneath the centre of the leafy target. Loshi rolled her eyes at the missed attempt.

"Loshi, you must concentrate." Hillius stood beside her in the archery garden. He handed her another arrow; she grabbed it, took a deep breath, and pulled back.

The arrow hit the second ring outside the target centre. The General flicked a clump of dirt at her, and she growled in frustration.

"Is it absolutely necessary to throw dirt at me? Today is an important day, I'm already anxious enough."

"I am well aware of the importance of your day, but my concern is your concentration and accuracy. Again."

Loshi drew back again, focused on the target and let go, missing the target completely. Her fists tightened and she hung her head in frustration.

"Ok, enough." He gave her a second to calm down.

"Steady your mind. Quiet your thoughts. Close your eyes, and feel the dirt hit you. Don't anticipate when the dirt will hit. Do not react," Hillius paused, then continued. "I understand you are nervous, Loshi. Take what's meaningful in everything that comes your way and learn from it. Absorb it, that's how you grow. Be calm and alert, smooth yet sharp, humble yet confident. Now, future Queen of the Adephaga, hit the centre of that target!"

She stood unflinchingly as the dirt and stones continued to hit her legs. She reached for another arrow and took aim, pulled back, and released.

Just as Loshi's arrow was about to pierce the centre, it was suddenly split in two by a second arrow, which seemingly appeared out of nowhere and then struck the centre target.

Loshi, first shocked and then angry, spun around to investigate the culprit. She looked up to see her mother at the bedroom window with her bow. The Queen smiled demurely and turned away, as Loshi shook her head in disbelief.

Loshi handed her bow back to General Hillius and grinned. "She still has it."

"She does," Hillius agreed, and smiled. He then looked at her squarely and placed his hands on her shoulders. "I wish you the best of luck today, Princess. Everything will be fine. It is up to you to choose how to handle what comes. It is either your blessing or your burden. It is time for you to live the life you were born to live...a life that many could only dream of. You understand?"

Loshi nodded and smiled softly, acknowledging her mentor's words. As she started back towards the palace, Aniya arrived to escort her back. She then stopped and pulled a spike from her bun; she spun around quickly and hurled it towards the tree, striking the centre of the target. She glanced at Hillius expectantly, who seemingly ignored her feat, but cracked a small smile as he walked away.

* * *

Trumpet flourish filled the air as the palace gates opened to receive the royal guests. Beetles dressed in their finest garments gathered for a chance to see some of the most esteemed members of the Adephaga and beyond - political figures, celebrities, military heroes, royal family and friends.

The place was abuzz as a regally dressed beetle stepped to the top of the stairs and cleared his throat, quieting the crowd.

"Hear ye, hear ye, beetles of the Adephaga and guests of the royal assembly, welcome. This evening we celebrate the coming-of-age of Princess Loshi. We also acknowledge and celebrate the continuous progress made by so many of those present here this evening, and of course a reminder of the sacrifices made by those who are no longer here with us. Ah yes, another reminder to all airborne beetles, please be safe and don't drink and fly. We don't want to relive last year's mishaps, and you know who you are."

A couple of the beetles in the audience look at each other and giggle as laughter spreads through the crowd.

"Now, without further ado, may I present our gracious hosts, his royal highness King Tearon and Queen Elytra!"

The crowd erupted in applause as the King and Queen entered the courtyard and descended the steps. The King's crown shone in the late evening sun. His coat was glossy and vibrantly red, embedded with crystals and adorned with spider fur around the collar and sleeves. Tearon raised his hands to quiet the crowd, and spoke proudly.

"My good and loyal beetles; tonight we share our food, our wine and our hospitality with you in gratitude. Our history teaches us that together, we are capable of great things. We have built a city of marvel; a city built on blood, sweat and tears. The beetles that lived and died building this Empire have not been forgotten; let us never forget, for they live in all of us. Because of perseverance, we are still here and we are stronger than ever. Above all, we are FREE!"

The guests cheered, whistled and roared. King Tearon looked to his Queen and she nodded her approval. The King stepped away and sat upon his throne. The Queen, ravishing in her beauty, stepped forward. Her dress was a deep luxurious shade of blue, adorned with golden lace. Her crown was delicate, and like the King's, dazzled brightly in the light.

"How lovely it is to have all of you here to celebrate three decades of peace and harmony among us beetles. Look at what we have created together through peace. It's truly magnificent. We are truly proud to lead the Adephaga into the future, and when the time is right, for our beloved daughter to carry on our legacy."

Loshi sat nervously behind the stage, fidgeting with her handkerchief as she awaited her name to be called.

"Sit still," Aniya whispered frustratingly as she stitched the finishing touches on Loshi's dress.

The Princess let out an exasperated sigh. "Forgive me, I'm just so nervous."

"Well if you don't calm down, I'll never get this -"

Just then the announcer pokes his bulbous head through the curtain. "Pardon me, but it is time, Princess."

Aniya scrambled to finish her task, and Loshi took a deep breath, awaiting her mother's introduction. Aniya took her hand.

"Don't be so nervous - you look beautiful! You're a special beetle, your mother laid over two hundred eggs and you're the only one that survived. I have a hundred and thirty four siblings, my parents stopped naming kids after eighty seven. Think about that! Your mom and dad named me when they hired me to keep you out of mischief."

Loshi smiled at her. "You're awful - a bad influence, and my only friend."

Aniya fluttered her long lashes at her and flashed a cheeky grin. The Queen was concluding her speech.

"As you all know, your Princess is at a desired age to wed, and thus we are seeking a suitor. We have chosen a beetle that we believe exhibits the noble qualities that would be suited for a Prince, and one day, a King."

The Queen pauses and looks at Tearon while all the beetles in the audience stood silently in anticipation. Off in the distance, the faint sound of galloping feet could be heard and began to rise in volume as it got closer. A rider entered the courtyard, attracting everyone's attention. The handsome beetle riding on the back of a full grown termite entered, parting the crowd. Guests watched in amazement as this striking beetle approached the throne; the termite lowered its torso for him to slide off. Never had any beetle seen a tamed and enslaved termite, so they cautiously kept their distance.

General Hillius ordered soldiers to stand on the four corners of the beast. The handsome beetle stepped toward the Queen and dropped to one knee.

"My gracious Queen, my name is Bruxis. I am the son of Lieutenant Zoiza and I have come in good will and courtship. The legions of beetles all speak highly of your daughter's beauty. Where is she, for my eyes to bear witness?"

The Queen turned to the King and he nodded. The Queen raised her hand and signaled the parting of curtains, revealing Loshi standing in all her beauty, frozen in fear. She was startled by Aniya nudging her forward, as the crowd whooped and clapped in admiration.

"Well, HELLO Sir Bruxis!" Aniya whispered from behind her.

Loshi shushed her, red-faced, as the King furrowed his brow at them. The Princess readjusted her ladylike poise as he stepped to her, taking her hand.

"Greetings, my fair Princess. I have traveled far to meet you."

Loshi was not easily impressed.

"And from where have you traveled from, Sir?"

"From far beyond these walls, my lady," Bruxis answered with a smile.

Loshi's eyes widened. "You live outside the Adephaga?"

Bruxis laughed softly, showing his unmistakable charm. "I do, and it would be an honor to show you my home. It is beautiful, though now I see its beauty is at no comparison to you."

Aniya stifled a giggle; Loshi stiffened at the sound, and the Queen herself struggled to maintain a straight face at Aniya. Loshi found herself feeling curious and mesmerized by this extraordinary beetle, despite her strong efforts to resist his advances.

A thunderous rumble from the termite cut the tension and startled the crowd. Nearby beetles nervously skittered away from it.

"Ah, my chariot has an appetite," Bruxis observed. The laughter from the crowd made Loshi smile and made her feel a bit calmer.

Suddenly, a loud bellowing horn cut through the air. The guests, startled, all turned to look in the direction of the sound. General Hillius, suspicious of what this was, signaled his two scouting beetles to climb to the top of the trunk to investigate.

Before they could reach the top, the scouts froze in horror as they saw a river of glass balls hurtling through the heavens towards them. Panicked, they ran back down towards the General, screaming their warnings incoherently.

As they reached the foot of the tree, the whistling grew louder and louder as two arrows perforated their backs and exited their chests. They dropped to the ground.

Chaos broke out as the crowd of beetles who had gathered in the palace scurried to safety. General Hillius, enraged, laid his hands on the two young beetles dead at his feet, and looked up at the walls.

"Shadow Beetles! Draw your swords and stand on guard, ready to protect and ready to fight!" The unseen camouflaged beetles opened their eyes, revealing themselves and ascending to the ground.

The ground began to shake as the General's soldiers raised the blockade to protect the court, readying themselves for what would surely be a bloody battle. Once erected, the soldiers stood silently; showing no fear, no emotion. Ready for war, ready for death.

Bruxis unsheathed his sword and stood beside King Tearon. "It is an honor to fight and defend you, O great King."

Tearon nodded slowly, pensively, as the walls began to crack and crumble. He knew they would not hold much longer against the sheer force of what was on the other side. They stood silent in the eerily quiet anticipation.

And then it happened. The walls came crashing down and a flood of D-Beetles poured into the palace, demolishing the blockade. The Shadow Beetles picked off their attackers deftly, fighting off beetle after beetle.

But the D-Beetles were relentless in their numbers and strength, and the Shadow Beetles became consumed and were soon overpowered.

The termite that had carried Bruxis had gone into an uncontrollable rage amidst the chaos of the battle, bucking and seething at the beetles surrounding it. Its chains rattled and then snapped, unleashing the savage beast as it tore through the soldiers on both sides indiscriminately.

After wiping out dozens of beetles in one fell swoop, the termite lurched slowly, menacingly, towards the throne. Before the termite could devour another soul, a Shadow Beetle leapt from a window overhead and unsheathed two swords in mid air, plummeting down and striking the termite through the head.

The D-Beetles seemed to pause in disbelief as the Shadow Beetle rose slowly, ready for attack. Out of the corner of its eye, the Shadow Beetle noticed the Queen, unseen amidst the mayhem, raising a trap door underneath the pulpit and rushing Loshi down into the hole. The Queen slipped in behind her and shut the door. Once it saw they had safely slipped to safety, the Shadow Beetle camouflaged itself and vanished.

* * *

Loshi felt her way down the staircase as she descended further into the hiding spot. She stopped abruptly. "Mother, we forgot Aniya!"

The Queen forcefully grabbed Loshi's arms, spun her around, and hissed, "There is no time! Follow the tunnel all the way - it will lead you to safety."

Loshi, fearful, gripped her mother's arm.

"I won't leave you!"

The Queen broke Loshi's grip. "My daughter, you are the love of my life. I need you to live. You must be brave, now go!"

The Queen climbed the stairs and pushed the trap door open, only to be grabbed and dragged out of the hiding spot. The surviving Adephaga beetles in the auditorium stood helpless and in fear as they were surrounded by D-Beetles, set for further carnage.

Hillius stood frozen with a blade held to his neck, staring helplessly at the countless number of dead soldiers. He closed his eyes; the blood dripping from his brow made a relentless tapping sound on his metal collar. He opened his eyes and stared coldly at Bruxis - a stare that made him visibly uneasy.

A D-Beetle stood tall and blew his horn, its deep bellowing sound echoed through the forest. The sun was setting on the Adephaga, and yet the battle had only just begun.

Part 4

The Rotting and the Wretched

he Queen stood off to the side, restrained by the D-Beetle guard, angry and visibly upset but trying to remain composed. King Tearon had kept his calm, but it was wearing thin. How was this possible in their kingdom? Who was responsible?

A final blow from the war horn echoed out, and the ground broke open. The Dark Lord Nicro emerged slowly from the dust and smoke. A terrifying sight, his armor steaming from the warmth of the earth. Soil crumbled off his armor built from skull and skeleton. His nightmarish mask concealed all but his enormous bloodshot eye.

The D-Beetles began to circle King Tearon, but were waved away by Nicro.

"Stay back. He is mine."

The King stood bravely as his ring began to glow and vibrate. He raised his hand to Nicro and the sword instantly appeared, mere inches from his face.

"Who are you to bring bloodshed and wrath into my kingdom?"

Nicro stepped closer to the tip of the King's sword, which lit up his mask eerily. "Like you, I am an orphan, born into the ashes of a father's legacy. I was born a King, an heir to a throne, a life one can only dream of. But instead, I was raised with indignity and savagery, baptized in the fires of hell. Our lives rotted underneath your feet, under your rule; watching you and your beetles live the life meant for us. Punished for the crimes of our fathers!"

Tearon stifled his intimidation. His sword still illuminated the fearsome mask of Nicro, so close that it began to burn Nicro's mask into his skin. As it smoldered, Nicro slowly and unflinchingly removes his mask, singeing his fingers as he did. A deep scar had formed across the right side of his face; his damaged eye appeared engorged, and it startled Tearon.

"Do I look familiar, King?"

Tearon, confused and at a loss for words, said nothing.

"Look at my face and tell me you don't remember!" Nicro roared.

Tearon did remember - how could he not? It was many years ago, but the memory, although buried deep in his psyche, was still there...

A young King Tearon stood braced against a wall, bewildered, as he watched the emergency medical beetles trying to revive a dead beetle lying on the floor by the dining table. An unknown young male beetle stood nearby, held by two guards, looking guiltily at the scene in front of him. A younger General Hillius stood by the King and cleared his throat. "We found him hiding in the kitchen, Your Majesty. We found your ring as well; he had stolen it, and we also found the poison he used in the attempt to take your life."

The young King confronted the scared young beetle. "Why did you try to kill me?" The beetle didn't utter a word; he just stared back at Tearon in anger.

The guard nudged him. "Your King has asked you a question, boy. It would be wise of you to answer." The young beetle still resisted. Tearon raised his voice, "I am your King! You must answer me!" He glanced over at his advisors as they nodded in approval. He slid his father's ring back onto his finger.

The beetle struggled against the grip of the soldiers, trying to free himself with all his might. Tearon wound up and backhanded the young beetle, slicing the side of his face with the ring's sharp edged stone. The beetle fell to his knees, screaming in agony while he covered his face. Blood slowly oozed through his fingers. Tearon stood over him, shocked by his own actions. The guards picked the still-screaming beetle up off the ground and dragged him away. Tearon, still frozen in disbelief, watched as the young beetle disappeared to an unknown fate.

Tearon gazed into Nicro's eye. "I remember you," he uttered quietly.

"But do you know who I am?"

Tearon warily eyed his challenger, not knowing his name but not daring to admit it.

Nicro inches closer with havoc in his eye.

"Your father once betrayed and killed his King in cold blood. I am the son of the one he murdered."

The King was at first taken aback, but his shock slowly turned to anger once he realized who he was. "Ediuss...you are the son of Ediuss. They say your father was a tyrannical leader, a ruthless dictator, and that his descendants were punished as retribution for your father's transgressions. You wanted to kill me...to avenge your father?"

"I was a small child, cast out of my own kingdom - blinded, abandoned and unwanted. I slaved and toiled away in the pits; once destined for greatness, I was instead forced to live my life in the dirt. A life that led me to crave the sweet release of death. But then, as I dwelled in the hollows underground, I was filled with renewed purpose. My struggles gave me the strength to live out my destiny. Now, I have come to help you meet yours, and take back what is rightfully mine."

The King was indignant at this threat, and raised his sword to aim at Nicro's other eye.

"I am no easy kill. Come, we shall see if I can take the other eye!"

Nicro stepped even closer to Tearon's sword, grabbing it tightly in his hand and licking it, splitting his wiggling tongue in two. Smoke began to pour from his burning hand, and with a mouthful of blood, he began to laugh sadistically - a frightening sight.

"It is not me who will take your life, your majesty."

Suddenly, the King's chest was perforated from behind by a large sword. The Queen cried out in horror and her knees gave way. Tearon stumbled, a wave of panic and agony washed over him as he gasped painfully. He turned slowly to see his assailant standing behind him - Bruxis.

Such betrayal! Queen Elytra shrieked as Bruxis pulled his weapon from the King's back, dropping him to the ground. Before she could move an inch, he bounded across the floor and held the sword across her neck, King Tearon's blood dripping onto her face, mixing with the tracks of her tears.

"Make one move, Your Highness, and I will cut you in two."

He pushed her to the floor beside Tearon's body, sobbing, struggling to hold him as his breaths grew more shallow. Nicro paused to observe his burnt hand with indifference, and then amusement. Observing the King crumpled into a bloodied ball with the Queen beside him, his shoulders began to shake with wicked laughter.

Nicro strode to the side of King Tearon, his eyes were two piercing daggers as he gazed upon Elytra. His sword was ready to strike, but he was unaware that she had quietly drawn a blade from his boot and slipped it into Tearon's right hand. Nicro grabbed Tearon's left arm and raised it up high, removing the ring from his finger and displaying it proudly for his army to see. They roared and stomped their feet in excitement so hard that the ground quaked beneath their feet.

Elytra and Tearon looked at each other without saying a word, but their eyes said everything. The stone began to pulsate and the light from Nicro's chest began to glow. Without a word, he opened his chest plate to reveal a necklace with the other stone attached. The two stones pulsed simultaneously, slowly gravitating to the other.

Just as the two stones were about to merge, Queen Elytra dove out of the way and Tearon, with the last bit of strength he had left, plunged the dagger into Nicro's leg, causing him to scream in pain. The ring flew out of his hand and landed a few feet away, in front of the trap door. Nicro backhanded King Tearon violently, causing him to roll off the platform and onto the dirt floor. Nicro snatched Elytra and held her so tightly from behind that she struggled to breathe, dragging his bleeding leg as he moved. He roared orders at his troops to look for the ring as they frantically scoped the area.

Seizing opportunity in the chaos, General Hillius wrapped his arms around the two opposing army beetles' heads and jerked them outward, breaking their necks. He grabbed both of their swords as they fell to the ground. He paused for a moment, and his eyes met Bruxis'. He rose to his feet, not breaking his gaze, ready to fight.

"Have you no honor, boy? To stab a King in the back and intimidate a Queen? Come, learn how to fight like a real beetle."

Hillius slowly circled Bruxis.

Nicro grabbed Elytra's face and forced it ahead. "Watch closely, my Queen... you won't want to miss this."

Bruxis gestured three large D-Beetles to attack Hillius. They slowly inched closer and closer to the General - he gripped his weapons tightly. They attacked all at once, slashing and stabbing, trying to overwhelm the General. Hillius dismantled them swiftly, one by one, until Bruxis raised his hand to cease the attack.

"Very impressive, General," He clapped obnoxiously. "You show great skill. I see fighting you the conventional way may not be sufficient."

Bruxis whistled a signal, and in mere seconds, and seemingly out of nowhere, a glass ball fell from the sky. He caught it in his left hand. Gently balancing the ball on the blade of his sword, he tossed it up with a flourish, and sliced it with the tip of his weapon, breaking it and splashing poison down the blade.

"Say your goodbyes, old beetle. Don't worry, this won't take long."

General Hillius rammed the two swords into the ground then knelt down, rubbing the cool dirt between his hands. He looked directly at his King and Queen as he rose up and retrieved his swords. He motioned for Bruxis to come to him, initiating what was sure to be a bloody combat.

Bruxis lunged forward, swinging his sword up and around, hitting Hillius' sword so hard that he went flying into the wall. Bruxis stood and flexed his giant body at him menacingly. He brought down his blade again as Hillius blocked and punched him in the jaw, causing him to fall back. Bruxis appeared pleased at this, and smiled as he spat out blood. Hillius blocked the next swing but crashed into a carriage, hurting him terribly. He caught his breath, his head buried into the earth. Hillius gathered his strength and began to crawl in pain as Bruxis moved closer for the kill; he picked him up and threw him into another wall, breaking it in pieces.

Unbeknownst to the combatants, soldiers, and prisoners, Loshi had crept up the hidden staircase, lifted the trapdoor, and was watching the events in horror. As Hillius hit the wall, she had winced and almost cried out. She looked to the ground beside him and saw her father still laying in a heap. She saw her mother shaking in fear as she watched her protectors being taken apart.

Just as she was about to retreat back down into her hiding place, she noticed the ring on the ground, just inches from the opening. She lifted the door high enough to grab it. Once in her hands, the ring began to glow brightly through the floorboards so she immediately hid it in the folds of her dress.

Bruxis walked over to Hillius and knelt beside him, placing the tip of his sword to his back.

"Please, no!" Elytra cried out, as Nicro nodded his approval. Bruxis plunged the poison-dipped sword all the way through the General, into the ground. Hillius' body gyrated in reaction, and his torso slowly began to smolder and mist. Everyone stood paralyzed in disbelief as he started choking and gasping, his outer skeleton slowly dissolving into dust amid the wind, blowing his ashes into the air. He looked pleadingly at Tearon as he slowly faded away to nothing.

Elytra and the others were traumatized at what they had witnessed. Never had they seen such horror and evil magic carried out before them.

Nicro shuffled through the puddle of King Tearon's blood and kicked his crown, splashing blood on some of the beetles. He turned to face Kring. "Roundup the children, collect the strong, kill the rest."

Tearon grabbed Nicro's ankle.

"Have you no mercy?!" he hissed, "let them live, you have defeated me. They have done no wrong against you."

Nicro grabbed Tearon's face so that he could look him square in his blind and scarred eye. "Were you merciful to me?"

Tearon closed his eyes in shame, knowing the answer needed not be spoken.

"I want this to be the last thing you see before your pathetic life is at an end. If you close your eyes, your Queen will join them."

The remaining Adephagan beetles began to panic as they were forcefully separated by D-Beetles. The unwanted beetles were herded into a circle in the centre of the grounds, nervously crying and whispering, awaiting their dreadful fates.

Once the beetles had been sequestered to Nicro's satisfaction, he glanced at Kring, who whistled up into the sky. Like tears from the heavens, an onslaught of poisoned spheres fell to the earth. As beetles screamed for their lives, Kring could not help but avert his eyes as glass balls dropped faster and faster, smashing all around the beetle civilians. The King cried out at the horrible sight as the screaming beetles slowly turned to dust.

Elytra struggled to break free."You monster! You know not what you have done!"

King Tearon, knowing he would not live much longer, protested further. "Have we not learned from the past? We have a code - no beetle shall kill another."

Nicro approached Tearon, kicking him over onto his stomach so that he was face down. "Tell your father that you have never seen evil as you did in the face of the man who took your life."

He pushed Tearon's face into the puddle as he struggled for air, but to no avail. Nicro drove his heel further onto Tearon's head, drowning him in his own blood, until his body stopped moving. Everything went silent.

"Noooooooo!"

The young Princess' desperate cry cut through the silence, startling everyone. The Queen quickly raised her head in panic. Nicro's eye widened as he turned to Elytra with a devilish grin.

"It's the child! She's beneath the floors! Get her!"

"Run!" screamed Elytra, as D-Beetles smashed through the floors haphazardly, trying to find the source of the sound.

Loshi was frozen in fear; she knew she had to move quickly, but for some reason, she couldn't put one foot in front of the other.

Suddenly, the trapdoor swung open. Loshi shielded her face instinctively, but was startled by Aniya pushing her further down the stairs and slamming the door shut behind her.

"Loshi, we must go!"

Aniya grabbed her hand; they stumbled and then ran through the tunnel as D-Beetles smashed through the trapdoor. Peering down the staircase, they saw the faint glow of the stone, jostling and growing smaller and smaller as the girls ran. The D-Beetles realized they had come across a tunnel and that Loshi had used it to evade capture.

A D-beetle looked up at Nicro. "My Lord, it seems she has escaped, and she has the stone." Nicro nodded pensively. "Find her alive, and kill any accomplices she may have."

He turned to Elytra, and put his giant hand around her throat.

"I want what is mine... your daughter's life means nothing to me."

Part 5

The Light in the Darkness

oshi and Aniya dashed through the dimly lit tunnel, their breathing becoming labored and their legs feeling heavier. The chaos that they had fled from seemed to be a safe distance behind them, so they slowed their pace slightly to catch their breath.

As they slowed, hearing the thumping of their heartbeats in their ears, they also began to notice a faint squeak that seemed to be coming out of nowhere, followed by a silent pause. They would hear it again, then a pause. Then again!

Aniya listened closer and her eyes widened when she realized the squeak sounded like a tiny voice calling to her each time they passed the lamps that were lighting their way.

"Stop...please...just a...wait..."

One of the little fireflies trapped in a lamp had seen them running toward him and began to make his light hypnotically strobe, closing his eyes and putting his hands out.

"You will pick up my cage...you cannot fight the urge to pick up my cage..."

Aniya snatched the lit lamp with the mighty little firefly inside.

"Ah ha!" he yelped, in a piercing, high-pitched squeak.

Suddenly, one of the D-Beetles that was still in pursuit a ways back roared, and it echoed throughout the tunnel: "There they are! Get them!"

The little firefly was startled and glanced up at Aniya.

"Set me free, and I will use my exquisite intellect and unparalleled fighting ability to help you get rid of those vicious creatures!" He flexed his muscles coyly, then launched into an elaborate demonstration of his fighting skills, ending in a mid-air Buddha pose.

"I also teach yoga."

Before the girls could react, a sword hurdled through the air and smashed into the wall, scattering dirt everywhere and shattering the firefly's antics. They turned a corner and Loshi looked back at the D-Beetles gaining on them, so close she could see the saliva dripping from their jowls.

"They're getting closer!" she shouted to Aniya.

Aniya looked to the little firefly in desperation, who stood bravely, ready to fight.

"Free me, and with my brothers and sisters, we will safeguard your passage. You have my word as a Thalmidian!"

Still running, Aniya shrugged and looked at Loshi who quickly nodded in agreement. She flung open the lantern and the firefly jumped out, twirling and somersaulting in the air, then giving her a little kiss on the nose.

"Liberty! Persist to the left, we will handle those hideous beasts."

The firefly flew off, unlocking lamp after lamp, prompting each firefly to flicker into action. The D-Beetles were practically on the heels of Loshi and Aniya when a small yet halting voice echoed through the tunnel...

"Sons and daughters of Thalmidia! We who bring fire to the night, shall taketh away!"

As if on cue, the fireflies' lights went out one by one; each lamp flickered and went out until they were under a blanket of darkness. The D-Beetles stopped dead in their tracks.

"Where did they go?"

"Silence! I see them!"

A faint green light ahead seemed to lead the way for the D-Beetles, showing the tunnel split into two passageways. The green light hovered straight for some time before veering slightly to the right. They tread cautiously towards the glow, making their way closer, when they began to hear crackling sounds under their feet.

One beetle spoke up nervously. "Sir...what are we walking on?"

His question was met with silence.

"Sir?"

"Never mind that! We must find her quickly or Nicro will have our heads," another beetle retorted impatiently.

Just then, a low and monstrous howl echoed through the tunnel and the D-Beetles all stopped dead in their tracks. One of the soldiers spoke up nervously, "Who goes there? Show yourself!"

Suddenly, the little green light they had been pursuing began to grow in size, becoming more illuminated and revealing a grisly image.

With a deep and horrid voice a warning echoed through the tunnel. "Fear me! Come any closer and you will pay with your blood," the giant silhouette seemed to bellow, which frightened the beetles enough to draw their swords in a panic. "Step no further, you unattractive, unmanicured heathens. Or else!"

The D-Beetles looked at each other the their hands in confusion.

The little firefly jumped out, surprising the beetles. "Ha! I have fooled you, because you are stupid"

The D-Beetles stared back in disbelief. "What's this, a flea?" Their snickers grew to laughter and they moved closer as the little firefly mimicked them, laughing back at them, then motioning for them to look down.

The glow of the firefly suddenly brightened to the fullest, exposing hundreds of spider eggs on the ground. The D-Beetles glanced at each other quietly and began to step backward slowly. The little firefly rubbed his back end, collecting fluorescent blue light, and then rubbed it on the left side of his face.

"Aye, fight and you will die, run and you will die. You may take our lights, but you will never take our freedom!"

Behind him, a large number of fireflies began to reveal themselves and their glowing bodies lighting up one by one. They spun around, shaking their illuminated back sides at them, taunting and yelling, causing a chaotic scene. In all the disruption, the D-Beetles were too distracted to notice the predator descending upon them from above - a menacing mother spider, moving in to protect her babies.

The anachroid descended slowly, moving closer and closer, quiet as death, completely unassuming, until two of the D-Beetles glanced up. What they saw made their eyes widen, and they shrieked in horror as she burst into attack.

* * *

The faint screams of terror echoed through the tunnel, alerting Loshi and Aniya. They paused and turned towards the sounds; the little firefly suddenly flew in between them, as if to sense their fear.

"You are safe from harm now, fair beetles. I will guide you the rest of the way."

"Who are you?" asked Loshi.

"I am Atero," he bowed his head in reverence. "Fear not, I may be exceptionally small but I make up for it with my outwittingness." Atero squinted his eyes in concentration and tapped his left temple.

"We were taken in our sleep during the day by these unfriendly and unfashionable looking creatures. It is my honor to repay the debt and protect you o' fair princess" Atero closes his eyes and bows.

Suddenly, Loshi began to weep. "He's gone. My father is gone and my mother... what will we do, we need to save her!"

Aniya hugged her tightly. "We will think of something, but for now we have to keep on moving."

Atero landed on Aniya's arm and peered up at Loshi. "Fear not fair Princess for you are safe as long as I am here."

Loshi raised her head and looked at him sullenly. "I was the bait used to kill my father and capture my mother. Now, they want this..." Her voice trailed off as she pulled out the ring.

Atero paused for a second, grabbed a drop of water from the moisture on the wall and used it as a magnifying glass. "Hello, beautiful!" He leaned in close to Loshi, "I have heard of this ring. It's very old, and very dangerous."

The ring began to glow its beautiful shade of green. Suddenly, out of the corner of her eye, Aniya noticed a mangled D-Beetle limping toward them. She grabbed Loshi's hand and they ran off. Atero grabbed a rock, rubbed it on his backend and threw it, hitting the beetle in his face and blinding him with florescent light. Atero took off behind Loshi and Atero, leaving the D-Beetle wincing in pain from the rock.

Within seconds, the pack of D-Beetles had caught up and ran past him as Bruxis stopped behind the battered beetle, who was still rubbing the light out of his eyes.

"Halt!"

The D-Beetles turned around, and the largest one roared, "They're getting away!"

Bruxis took a handful of the iridescent light off the beetles face. "Soldiers - hand me your blades."

He rubbed the tips of all their swords and the same light emanated from them.

Bruxis looked down at the Beetle dying in his arms, and then looked at the other beetles. "Forget your orders; when we find them, we will show them the same mercy they have shown our friend Balidor."

The D-Beetles growled, nodded in agreement and took off down the tunnel. The D-Beetle died in Bruxis's arms as his anger become more furious.

* * *

Further in the tunnel, Loshi stopped abruptly in her tracks as if something had hit her out of nowhere.

"Wait...I have been here before! There should be a hidden passage somewhere here that leads back to the library." Loshi began feeling her way around the walls frantically.

"My father and I used to play hide and seek when I was younger - I used to always hide in the study," she stammered. "One day, I was curious about one of the books on the shelf. I went to pull it out, and the entire mantelpiece opened and it leads to this corridor, I am sure of it! Somewhere here..." her voice trailed off.

Loshi gently took Atero in her hand, using his warm glow as a flashlight, as her hand grazed over a wooden surface inconsistent with the dirt of the tunnel.

"I think this is it."

She felt for the latch, pulled open the little hidden wooden door, and slipped into the wall.

Part 6

Raindrops Keep Falling on the Dead

W hether one believes in fate or luck, both are equally powerful forces. And as luck, or fate, would have it, it started to rain. To many, this rain may not seem important - a simple, predictable act of Mother Nature. But for the beetles, rain is especially perilous due to the simple fact that the Adephaga floods easily. And as the all too familiar phrase goes - when it rains, it pours.

The Adephaga was designed with natural drainage openings at all four corners of the land that were only opened during the rainy season. They provided a type of irrigation system that would help the water to drain out, but this rain was out of the ordinary.

As the rain came down, Nicro's entire fleet was now above ground and moving Beetles to sectioned camps in the schools. He sat on his new throne watching and listening to the muffled cries of beetles being forced out of their homes. Queen Elytra sat on the floor bound beside him, tied up and visibly shaken from witnessing the carnage that had unfolded at the hands of Nicro. Two D-Beetles entered and knelt before him, breathing heavy from the hunt.

"Lord Nicro - we have chased them through the tunnels, within the walls, there is no way out and yet they are gone."

Bruxis stepped behind the soldiers in an act of validation. "What they say is true, Father. This can be verified, they serve you honorably."

Nicro turned to face Elytra, who appeared relieved at the report. "Those tunnels must lead somewhere, look again! The girl must be found!" His glare at the nervous D-Beetles intensified. "Do not come back empty-handed."

Bruxis approached Nicro and whispered in his ear, "We cannot go back down there, Father. It's flooded"

Suddenly, Kring entered the room abruptly accompanied by two D-Beetles interrupting Bruxis. "We have a severe crisis my Lord; your attention is needed at once."

Nicro placed his hand on Bruxis' shoulder. "Take the Queen to the palace chambers and have two guards watch her. She is not to be left alone."

Bruxis glanced at the Queen smugly. "Yes Father, as you wish." He nodded to the D-Beetles, who unlocked Elytra and roughly lifted her to her feet before dragging her off the podium.

Kring continued with nervousness. "The beetles you desire have been gathered and the others were executed as you asked, my Lord. But, the rain is causing flooding in the southwest corner of the land and is quickly rising. We fear this rain will not let up. We must move to higher ground."

Nicro gazed out the window silently for a moment before addressing Kring.

"Move the women and children to the school auditorium with the rest. Have the men build rafts. If they want to live, they will live as slaves. A little rain will not spoil my chances of recovering the stone."

"Yes my Lord, at once." Kring bowed and stepped away.

* * *

A small wooden door in the palace library opened slightly. Atero peered out from behind it to survey the room. Once he saw that the coast was clear, he darted out and flew haphazardly from corner to corner and all over, looking everywhere for any signs of danger. His eyes fell upon a garden worm slowly moving across the floor. He squinted hard at it. "I can never tell which end is which." He flew back to the ajar door and hovered bravely over them. "It is safe, for now."

Loshi and Aniya ran to the study room window and looked out at the intense rain. Aniya stuck her head out to investigate, before recoiling quickly. "I've never seen such a rainfall! We are not prepared for a storm like this."

Loshi noticed a woman and children being forced into the school by a D-Beetle soldier. "If they are moving beetles above ground, the water levels must be rising quickly."

Atero flew to the door and paused. "I will search the area for heathens." He dove under the door only to fly right back in, landing with his back against the door and his arms out in a complete fright.

"Ok, time to panic! We are surrounded and they have a beetle-sniffing termite!"

The girls gasped quietly and held their breath, as they realized what that meant. In the silence of the room, the sound of sniffing on the other side of the door made everyone freeze in fear.

"The beast smells something in here," muttered a low gravelly voice. The sudden sound of the doorknob rattling cut through the silence as the D-Beetles tried to unlock the door. The King had kept his study locked, but the girls knew it would only be a matter of seconds before the soldiers made it through.

"It's locked. Stand clear, I'll break it down."

Atero whispered to Loshi, "This is it - we must jump out the window, it is a better death than being eaten by the termite. They over chew their food it is disgusting!" He looks her in the eyes and dry heaves as Loshi looked down in fear.

Suddenly, they heard a loud BANG! The soldiers had begun to ram the door in an effort to knock it through.

BANG! BANG!

Aniya grabbed Loshi's arm. "We must hide! Quick, back into the tunnel." They scurried back to the wooden door and slid in quickly as Atero looked around frantically. His eyes fell upon a wet bar and in an instant, he had an idea.

BANG!

He flew to the bar just as the door crashed open. The termite bounded into the room, dragging the two D-Beetles behind it, only to find Atero quickly flipping and tossing bottles around. Remembering the green worm, he swooped down to grab the little grub from the ground, dropped it on the bar and reached for a large knife. The little grub looked back at him with sad little eyes, mouth quivering in fear.

"I'm sorry little friend, but it's for the greater good. Now, slither towards the light."

With that, he chopped the insect in half and flung each piece into the termite's mouth as it dropped to the ground, chewing away. The two D-Beetles stood bewildered at the strange sight in front of them. "Well, howdy boys! You're just in time, I'm about to make my world famous Ugondie cocktail. A tasty little treat my granddaddy used to make, it will blow your taste buds right outta your eyeballs!"

As Atero continued his excessive bar flair, the soldiers looked over at the termite who seemed to be sleeping peacefully on the ground. They glanced at each other, shrugged their shoulders, and sat at the bar. Atero placed the drinks in front of them.

"Ooooo wee, I'll be a caterpillar's fuzzy backside if ya'll don't think this is the best drink you ever had. Drink up, boys!"

The D-Beetles grabbed their mugs and drank them back quickly, clearly delighted by these libations. "Not bad at all," exclaimed one of the soldiers.

"Didn't I tell ya? Well how 'bout another round, boys? On the house!"

The one soldier looked at the other and slammed his hands on the bar. "We work so hard, and never a thank you! Never a *good job, Melorok!* or *your killing quota is exceptional, Melorok.*" The other Beetle nodded in agreement.

Atero put the next round of drinks down in front of them and stood back, waiting in anticipation, nibbling on his fingertips. The beetles clashed their mugs together, yelling out "Arak Runda Beurrah!" and drank them back again, slamming their empty mugs on the table. They laughed merrily as they draped their arms around each other's shoulders. As their laughter died down, one of the soldiers let out a loud fart and grinned in embarrassment.

His smile quickly turned to confusion as he suddenly went limp, keeled over and slumped to the ground. Melorok looked at his fellow soldier in horror,

41

then at Atero in rage, gripping his sword. He opened his mouth to speak, only for his tongue to fall out and splatter onto the bar. Falling backwards off of the stool, he began convulsing on the ground, squirming in agony as Atero slowly peers over. Guiltily, he holds a bottle of liquor in one hand and a bottle of poison in the other. "Uh oh... these bottles are so confusing." The beetle lurched up, then gargled out his last breath.

Atero flew over to the termite and landed on his side. He leapt up and landed hard onto the beast, as blood squirted out of its mouth. Atero stood heroically with his hands perched atop his sides, gazing to the heavens. "I'm very good."

Once the chaos seemed to have calmed, Loshi and Aniya slowly opened the wooden door and ran in soaking wet to find Atero laying on the dead termite's body, celebrating with a fancy cocktail. He looked at them suavely, squinted his eyes and tapped the side of his head, again.

* * *

The Queen sat sullenly, staring out the window, ignoring the two soldiers stationed in her room. She watched as the body of her dead husband floated below, along with many others, in the half-flooded courtyard.

The door swung open and Bruxis strode into the room. Elytra's heart filled with rage at the mere presence of him, yet she didn't break her gaze from the window. "Your father's plan will fail; the rain will kill us all. All of this was for nothing."

Bruxis made his way over to the window slowly, stepping up behind Elytra. She still refused to look at him, she would not give him the satisfaction of seeing her in fear. Her body clenched up in dread as he slowly slid his hand up her back, then gripped her neck, lifting her effortlessly off the ground. She squirmed and thrashed violently, trying to free herself as he turned her to face him. He looked deep into her eyes and smiled.

"You don't know, do you? You're so innocent and sheltered in your big tree trunk. Your end was inevitable."

Elytra, unable to speak and practically suffocating, was forced even closer to him. He leaned in, sniffed her slowly and whispered, "The stones will change the prophecy." She looked at him with confusion for mere seconds before he suddenly dropped her, and she collapsed to the ground. Bruxis leaned his arm into her head and pushed it to the ground, forcing Queen Elytra to close her eyes and clench her teeth in pain. He placed his head beside hers. "Soon we will find her, and she will suffer. We will stop at nothing, even if it means taking her precious little life." Bruxis smiled as Elytra grit her teeth in pain.

Just then, a D-Beetle entered the room abruptly. "Excuse my intrusion, Sir, but you are needed at once!"

Bruxis glared up at the beetle, annoyed by the intrusion, and let go of the Queen as she lands back down hard on the ground. As he walked towards the door, he glanced back at her laying in agony and then up at the guards "Watch her closely and wait for my word," he instructed.

* * *

The male beetles worked relentlessly, building massive rafts with layers of sticks, twigs and leaves. The poisonous glass balls were carefully tied to the sides of the rafts to help keep them afloat. The cold rain stung their wound without mercy by D-Beetle Commanders. Nicro stood watching triumphantly as his army's production impressively installed giant nets to the rafts. The rafts were soon completed, commended and boarded.

In the midst of this, Bruxis approached Nicro. "Father, the water has reached the castle and has begun compromising the structure of the palace. I am not sure how long the foundation will hold. Also, the girl has not been found and the troops we sent have not come back."

Nicro removed the necklace from around his neck, pulling out the green stone, admiring its beauty. An overwhelming, unnatural obsession with its power. He looked at bruxis with a cold stare that could freeze the sun. "Check again." fear consumed Bruxis's face as he nodded and left, signaling troops to follow. He and his squad entered the palace, which was flooded knee deep with water. They made their way down the halls, searching each room left and right. Once they reached a split in the hallway, Bruxis motioned for the two D-Beetles to go right as Bruxis started down the hall to the left.

He had made it about halfway when he noticed that a doorway up ahead had been smashed in. He paused to listen, then unsheathed his sword and moved slowly into the room.

Once inside the room, he was shocked to find a small wooden door behind a bookshelf that was open, revealing a tunnel, and the two dead D-Beetles lying on the floor by the bar.

High above Bruxis, Loshi, Aniya and Atero hid in the giant chandelier that was hoisted high into the ceiling. They peered over, deathly afraid and being careful not to make a sound as they all knew what would happen if they were discovered. Sure enough, the ceiling made a cracking sound, loud enough to alert Bruxis, and he looked around the room slowly.

"Is that you Princess? Don't be afraid, I won't hurt you," he called out soothingly. Aniya looked at Loshi and shook her head slowly and firmly.

All of the sudden, the ring began to glow. Loshi covered her hand quickly as the ceiling cracked again and the chandelier dropped lower. Bruxis looked up quickly and growled as he took a swing at the chandelier. He smashed the bottom end, sending pieces of glass flying everywhere, and then his eyes locked on Loshi.

"I've been looking for you, Princess."

Aniya held on to Loshi tightly as Bruxis extended his hand."Throw me the ring, and I will spare you all." Loshi looked at the ring, and then back at Aniya, seemingly contemplating his promise. Aniya shook her head again as Atero flew onto the top of the chandelier and held onto its chain. He looked at Bruxis with a mischievous smile and called out, "We will never surrender to you!"

He locked eyes with Bruxis, both waiting in anticipation of who would make the first move. Bruxis swung his sword, and Atero snapped the chain; the giant chandelier dropped and crashed on top of Bruxis into a thousand pieces.

As if on cue, the palace walls, softened by the rain, brake apart and smash into the water creating a tidal wave. The broken chandelier is pushed by a wave of water and shoots out of the place. Nicro, who stands in shock, watches as the chandelier crashes down and sails downstream out of sight. Then, he suddenly noticed Bruxis floating in the water, motionless. He let's out a roar, and jumps in to pull him out.

Nicro laid Bruxis out onto one of the rafts; he put his head to his son's torso, but there was no movement. Nicro pierces Bruxis' chest with his long sharp talon, and water spewed out of his lungs and mouth. Seeing the inevitable, Nicro clutched Bruxis to his chest and let out a roar. He looked at Kring in despair as rain and tears poured off his face. With madness in his eyes, he shouted, "Send out your air fleet, I want them dead!"

Without missing a beat, Kring ordered his troops to gear up. He sliced the nets holding the poisoned glass balls and tossed one to each soldier. One by one, they caught the balls, fastened them into their chest pieces and took off into the sky.

* * *

The chandelier slowly sailed on, with Loshi, Aniya and Atero still atop it. They all watched in despair as they passed monuments and landmarks completely submerged. The beautiful Adephaga was almost unrecognizable. The sound of rain hitting the swells of the flood water was like a kind of depressing white noise as they drifted further and further away from home.

Amid the rushing water, Atero heard a humming in the sky. He lifted his head to investigate above them. Nothing. Yet the humming was distinct, growing slightly louder each moment. He flew up a ways to get a better view.

"Do you hear that? Is there a sound in the sky?"

Loshi looked up at him bleakly. "All I hear is the rain."

Aniya furrowed her brow, then pointed up. "There is something behind those clouds... look!"

Suddenly Atero's body began to glow violently, like an alarm. "Look out!"

A ball dropped to the right of them, missing them by mere inches, smashing and fizzing in the water. The air fleet sped closer and closer, shooting arrows and poisonous balls at them. An arrow came so close to Loshi's face that she felt its breeze before Aniya caught it. Loshi looked at her in disbelief.

The flood waves swirled and shifted them in different directions, making them a hard target. An arrow hit the metal arm of the chandelier, causing more shards to break off. Aniya snatched up a piece to use as a shield to protect them. Atero struggled with his soaked wings and climbed on Aniya's shoulder. His body began to flicker alarmingly. "They're gaining on us!"

Loshi arose slowly with tears in her eyes, standing brave, like her father did. "Loshi, no!" Aniya cried desperately and reached for her.

The D-Beetles hurtled towards them, winding up their swords as she held firm. Loshi slid the glowing ring onto her finger, and the sword appeared in all its glory. Atero shook and flapped his wings, and flew up into the sky, making target rings with his light.

Suddenly, Loshi began to feel the sword change shape and mould into a magnificent bow. She touched the string and an arrow appeared. She pulled back and fired a beautiful shot, hitting a D-Beetle as he collided into three others, plummeting them into the water.

Atero flew back from the power of the shot like a blast from a cannon and spiraled back down to the girls. His eyes widened as he looked ahead, seeing a waterfall was coming closer and closer as the water was picking up speed. He looked back at them in a panic. "Hold on for your lives, we're going over!"

Aniya grabbed Loshi and wrapped herself tightly to the chandelier. The second fleet of D-Beetles looked down at the chandelier speeding closer to the edge. "They are going over, look!" one of the soldiers alerted.

They slowly tipped over the side of the tree trunk and disappeared out of sight. They plummeted down, eventually crash landing onto a branch. Atero ran his hands over his wings and body, ensuring everything was intact.

He gave them a look of relief when all of a sudden, the branch began to shake. They looked up to see a massive rush of dirt and stone smash into the tree, the impact making the branch reverberate and knocking the chandelier over, plunging them all into the surging tide. The chandelier whipped and whirled through the mudslide picking up speed quickly. They slid down the hill and eventually off a cliff, free falling down and smashing into a flower garden.

Overhead, the D-beetles stopped and hovered over the waterfall. "There is no surviving a fall like that. They are surely dead. We will go back and inform Nicro." They turned around and flew off.

Part 7

Plummeting Over the Edge of Tomorrow

A young Loshi and her father walked through the forest on a beautiful sunny afternoon. The sky was a brilliant shade of blue, and the faint chirps and buzzes of all in the Adephaga could be heard. Suddenly, a scream cut through the calm; they rounded the corner to investigate the sound and stumbled upon a hornet cornering two young beetles who were walking home from school.

The hornet moved closer, intimidating the scared little beetles. "Don't be scared, little children," the hornet whispered, "I won't bite..."

Tearon guided Loshi back behind a shrub for her safety and stepped behind the giant hornet, who noticed his presence and turned his head slightly.

"Mind yourself, beetle...I'm about to have my dinner," he murmured, clearly not recognizing the King, who stood still and calm.

"You have no business in the Adephaga. Our species have agreed to an oath."

The hornet revealed his sharp black stinger, and looked at the King with eyes of madness.

"I made no such oath."

He steps closer, pausing to gaze upon Loshi behind the shrub. He grinned devilishly.

"When I am done with these two, she will be dessert."

Tearon's ring began to glow, surprising the large hornet as he stumbled back. The magnificent green translucent sword appears in his hand. Seeing this, the hornet lunged at the King, who swiftly swung his sword, slicing the tip clean off the hornet's stinger.

The hornet paused in shock, his mouth agape at the tip of his stinger on the ground. He glowered at Tearon and screamed out hysterically as he held his tip-less stinger.

"You monster! How am I going to explain this to my parents?? You just ruined my life," he sobbed. "Who is gonna want a hornet with a stub for a stinger!"

Loshi watched in confusion as the hornet grabbed his stinger tip off the ground and flew away sobbing. The two young beetles ran up and hugged Tearon.

"Now, now, little ones, run home to your parents. Go."

They ran off as he walked toward Loshi, who just stared at her father in shock, making him smile.

"You know magic? Teach me, Father! Please! I will be the greatest sorceress the world has ever known!" She waved her hands as if to cast a spell, making Tearon laugh. "I am no wizard, Loshi, and the magic is not from myself." He removed the ring and handed it to her.

"This is the ring of Kings. It's passed down from king to king, ruler to ruler. My father took it from the wretched Ediuss and it was passed down to me from him. You will be the first Queen to carry the stone one day. It is your destiny. Deep in our history, wars have been waged and beetles have killed for it. The stone is Jakiko, or God Stone, and it has siblings, whose whereabouts are unknown. It carries a special magic and it serves who wears it. A deadly weapon."

Loshi looked at the ring and then back at the King quizzically.

"It becomes a part of you and when your life is threatened or when you are most vulnerable, it comes to life," Tearon explained. "There is no defense, no struggle, there is only death."

* * *

Loshi awoke to the rain slowly washing the dirt off her bruised and battered body. She slowly opened her eyes and blinked away the blurriness as the sound of raindrops rolling off the leaves and tapping onto the ground seemed to pound like drums in her head. The clouds began to lighten as the rain slowly dissipated. The winds began to calm. She thought about her dream and looked down at the ring with tears in her eyes.

Loshi glanced at Atero and Aniya, who still lay unconscious, Atero's light flickering in and out like a dying flashlight. She rose to her feet and slowly walked through the broken chandelier pieces scattered everywhere. She looked up, trying to see past the fog to the top of the trees, amazed at how she survived the fall.

At that moment, she caught the scent of something burning, woody and sweet. She looked up to see a giant butterfly perched up under a big leaf. He sat there sheltered from the rain with his legs crossed, smoking a cigar and reading a newspaper on the back of a palm leaf. His wings were black and white striped, and his hair was streaked grey at the sides. Sensing he was being watched, he folded down the top of the newspaper, revealing his a bushy mustache and fuzzy eyebrows.

"You better get out of here, see, if you know what's good for ya," his cigar bobbed up and down as he spoke. "Surviving a fall like that? Pfft! You're gonna run outta luck, kid!"

Loshi looked at him pleadingly. "Please sir, can you help me? We were being chased and..."

A loud hissing sound interrupted her and she stopped to look around. The butterfly folded his paper and flicked his cigar, putting it back in his mouth.

"You look like a good kid, so I'm gonna give you some advice. Forget where ya came from, forget what you know. It's all about survival out here, doll face."

A loud hissing sound startled her again and she covered her hand as the ring began to vibrate. The butterfly flapped his wings and floated up with a grin.

"Good luck kid, you're gonna need it."

"Please help us, don't leave!" Loshi called out desperately.

He gave her a wink and took off, leaving Loshi alone. A cold shiver came over her as she began to hear whispers.

"Saaacuuuurraaaa..."

She begins to see white streaks, like lightning, zooming through the green forest as the whispers came closer and closer.

"Saaacuuuurraaaa..."

Out of nowhere, she was startled by the tip of a long spear emerging from the forest, which appeared to be aimed directly at her face. She raised her hands as more long spears began to emerge slowly out of the flowers and leaves. A savagely rugged voice suddenly echoed through the landscape.

"Buru Aruntia Condor!"

Instantly, every single spear aimed at her moved an inch closer, making it impossible for her to budge. She stood still as mysterious eyes began to appear in the green darkness. A large silhouette emerged through the ruffling leaves, but the mist and fog made it difficult for Loshi to see clearly. Slowly, a face suddenly appears, white as snow with bleeding red eyes, hovering toward Loshi.

She became frightened as it unsheathed two daggers and held them tightly with the presumption of danger. Ready to attack, he came closer, letting out a roar that shook the ground. Loshi's eyes rolled back as she collapsed to the ground, unconscious.

* * *

A young white beetling ran his fingers across her cheek in an attempt to rouse her. He looked up to the tribal leader saying softly "Saranuna noirru?" The little beetle puts out his hand for all to see and smiled "Siafti Purru!"

All the other beetles hummed and nodded as they stared in wonder at their discovery. The white beetle knelt beside her peacefully as Loshi's eyes fluttered open.

She sat frozen in fear, then in wonderment, at what lay before her. She analyzed him carefully, confused by what he was, as he appeared savage and wild. His body was a powdery ivory with grey spotted designs on his shell that gleamed against the overcast sky.

He had two bright red streaks painted under both eyes and tribal markings on all his limbs. His neck and chest were scarred with a slight chip on the right of his back shell. He looked around at the broken chandelier pieces and Loshi pointed up the tree trunk.

"We fell and crashed. My friends need help, please..."

He stood mystified and put his daggers away, turning his head back and raising his hand.

"Aturra kupa!"

Quickly dozens of spears pulled back as the white beetle waved them forward. One by one, the tribal beetles came out of hiding, all with different colors of war paint on their faces and bodies.

Just then, Aniya began to wake and slowly sat up. Her eyes adjusted to what was happening; she appeared confused and uncomfortable. She slowly climbed to her feet, not aware that all eyes were on her as she pulled a pin out of her mud soaked hair and shook it out.

"Ugh...someone's gonna pay for this! I spent a fortune on this tarantula weave!"

The white beetles looked upon her in attraction and intrigue as they laid their weapons down, chanting "Chuntah, Siafre Chuntah."

Aniya looked at Loshi, then at the white beetles, and then back at Loshi and whispered, "are we....dead?"

Atero began to mumble " No you are attractive, no no no... ok I am. Yes the cheek bones run in the family." He jolted up instantaneously, clearly emerging from a dream.

The white beetles giggled as he looked around at them. Perplexed, he rubbed his eyes and looked at the tribeetles again, falling to his knees in shock. "Why! I'm so young, and so very handsome. I don't remember seeing a white light."

Loshi ran to Aniya and hugged her tight. "I was so worried! Are you hurt?"

She looked herself over in amazement. "I seem to be in one piece...where are we?"

"I don't know but, I don't feel we are in danger," Loshi shrugged.

Atero admired himself as he looked at his reflection in a puddle. "Even dead, I'm very desirable!"

The tribeetles begin to move through the sparkling blades of grass, motioning for the three friends to follow. The light rain shimmered like diamonds as water ran down the green shafts. The sound of children laughing and playing grew louder as they came closer to what appeared to be a village. As they approached, they were immersed in an astonishing array of colors.

Luscious, vibrant flowers, with beautiful bleeding hearts that had been made into homes. Exotic dahlias and bluebells of all sizes grew lushly and ubiquitously, and were used in their hair and clothes. Their markings were unique and colorful against their pale white bodies. Beetles cooked on spits and others carrying on their daily duties stopped to stare at their new guests.

Loshi saw the familiar white beetle walk towards her. He approached and dropped to his knee, putting his head down and his hand to his chest. "Siaffre pall, noirru kweesa."

A beautiful female with delicate flowers woven into her hair and dress came to his side, putting her hand on his shoulder.

"His name is Teok, the son of Athiok. I am his sister Athara; we are of the Asunta tribe. We have waited for this day."

Aniya and Atero stood in awe of her beauty as she held out her hands to Loshi. All the white beetles bowed to her. She smiled and picked one of her flowers sewn in her hair, placing it into Loshi's.

"Am I dreaming?" Loshi asked softly.

The beautiful beetle moved closer. "This is no dream child, but I have seen you in mine."

Loshi was surprised at this. "I can understand you."

The white beetle smiled. "I learned your language a long time ago, as long as I've been looking for that stone. For all of ages, my people have prayed to the Gods that a beetle would bring us hope. You carry the Jakiko stone. It is the missing piece to our lost history and the link between our worlds."

Loshi listened in wonderment.

"It was once a star that died years before our kind. Found by our forefathers and used for power and greed. It runs in your blood as well as ours. Tell me, where did you get this stone?"

Loshi's eyes filled with tears as she stared at the ring. Aniya and Atero lowered their heads as she observed Loshi's sadness, and embraced her.

"You need not answer. Come now...you have been through a great deal, we will talk of this another time. Go and rest now; tomorrow you will meet Father." Two female beetles approached and took Loshi and Aniya to a stream to clean the mud off themselves.

As they made their way to the stream, Athara gazed in their direction.

"The words of Jakima are real. We will now fulfill the prophecy. She has come to save us. My intuition tells me she is being hunted, for the stone I presume."

Teok stood tall and looked over at Loshi at the stream, and then looked back at Athara. "Then we will protect them." A look of concern washed over Athara's face as Teok walked away.

Part 8

The Prey and the Prophets

The rain finally slowed to a windy mist as the air fleet arrived back at the palace. Nicro sat staring at the corpse of his son laid out on a table. He turned his head slightly as guards walked in behind him.

"Where are they?"

A soldier beetle stepped up. "They are surely dead, my Lord. They fell over the edge of the waterfall."

Nicro turned around, grabbing the beetle by the throat and squeezing tightly. "Did you fly down and check to see if they are dead? Did you retrieve the stone?"

The beetle looked at him wide eyed in fear, not saying a word. Nicro's grip tightened, squeezing harder until a sickening CRACK sound was heard. The beetle crumpled to the floor.

Enraged, Nicro picked him up over his head and smashed him back to the ground as the other D-Beetles looked on in horror. He collapsed at the side of Bruxis and let out a pained roar as the D-Beetles stood back, trembling in fear. He glared at them, breathing deeply with fire in his eye.

"Gather our armies. We are going to find that girl, and the stone!"

* * *

The day's dampness and soft breeze filled the air with floral delights as Aniya and Loshi followed Teok through the village. Atero flew around in amazement, catching a whiff of something delicious in the air.

"That is a wonderful aroma! I must investigate."

Aniya nudged Loshi, "Can you believe this place? White beetles, tribes? Isn't it like we went back in time a million years?"

Aniya stared at Teok as he walked ahead of them. "And handsome beetles, too!"

Loshi rolled her eyes as Aniya continued. "Teok is kinda cute in a sexy primal *'I'll hunt food for your love'* sort of way."

Loshi's face went red with embarrassment. "Shhh! Stop it, he can hear you."

Teok smirked to himself as he led them to a little flower hut. They swished through a cascade of daffodils that seemed to stretch for miles until they reached a grassy hill. The hill was so high, the morning mist covered the top. As they moved upward, the grass faded to soil as hundreds of cherry tomato plants consumed the landscape.

They were soon greeted by an elderly male tribeetle. His face was handsomely aged with light blue markings that followed down his chest and arms. His eyes were a rare crystal blue color that made it hard not to stare deep into them. He puts out his hands in the way that a cheerful grandfather would.

"Junto abrodia, welcome!" He looked Loshi up and down, shaking his head. "We both beetles, but you are very different, yes? You had quite the fall, who chase you?"

The old beetle giggled jovially. He then took Aniya's hands and looked at her, examining her plumpness as he poked at her sides. He then noticed the male beetles staring at her while the females looked at them with jealousy. He laughed, shaking his head and looking at the crowd of female beetles.

"Froentia chunta, pouentu orias." The girls looked at each other and giggled, then ran up to Aniya, grabbing her hand and taking her with them.

Just then, Atero flew up to them, appearing distressed as his light flickered on and off. The old tribeetle looked at Loshi and shrugged his shoulders, then looked at Atero and smiled.

"Ahh very unique creature, yes? I see you are very clever and brave, eh mister?"

Atero nodded slowly and squinted his eyes. "You are a very wise old beetle... tell me more."

The old beetle giggled, put his fingers on Atero's stomach, and the light flickered. The old beetle stopped and thought a while, tapping his lip. He looked at the beetle to his side.

"Ella briat o druvasta." The tribeetle walked a few feet, took a red sack from his pouch and tied a long thread to it, tying the other end around his wrist. He took his arrow and pierced the sack, then shot it straight up to the sky until the string stopped. The red sack tore open, making a red powdery explosion in the sky. Within seconds, a gorgeous orange and pink firefly with golden yellow markings soars over to them. Atero stood shocked at the firefly's beauty as it landed by the wise tribeetle flapping its lavish eyelashes. He grabbed a flower from Loshi's hair and handed it to the firefly.

"Hello my beautiful! My I say, you are irresistible!"

The firefly frowned angrily and slapped Atero in the face with his wing. "My name is Rok and I'm a guy, buddy! Why does everyone always think I'm a girl? I'm getting sick of it!"

Atero stood dazed as the old beetle and Loshi laughed.

"I think because you are pink!"

Rok's eyes bulged in disbelief. "How dare you, I am the color of hell fire! Insects quiver at the sight of me!"

Atero looked at Rok and bowed respectfully.

"I apologize, Sir...please forgive me, I meant no disrespect. My name is Atero and I am a Thalmidian."

Rok paused skeptically, and then nodded.

"I'm a Druvastian, I guess that makes us... cousins. Let's go see if we can get you back up to speed; follow me."

As he flew off, Atero looked at the Loshi. "Who knows, maybe he has sisters." He winked and took off through the blades of plant leaves and up into the sky.

Aniya reemerged dressed in the floral garments of the female tribeetles. Loshi looked at her with surprise "Wow, Aniya!"

Aniya twirled around with joy, "I could get so used to this! And I smell great. Come get dressed up too!"

The female tribeetles waved them over. They ran off, and the wise old beetle turned to Teok.

"How amazing. Beetles like us, but not us. We are different in color, but not so much in here," he touches Teok's chest.

"They have been through a great struggle," Teok replied with concern.

"She carries the Jakiko Stone, it protects her," said the wise beetle, nodding in acknowledgement. "A gift from the Gods, yes?"

Teok nervously shook his head. "She knows not its power, she brings danger to us. I feel it, they are scared."

The aged beetle looked up at Teok. "Wherever there is the Jakiko, there is blood. She is here for purpose. We are at the brink of war, the Gods have sent us a weapon."

Teok appeared pensive as the female beetle dressed up Loshi.

"What they are scared of comes for them."

The old beetle laughed and said, "They will not have an easy passage, the frogs will make sure of that. A message has already been sent. We feast tonight, tomorrow we go to Eboulo Mountain. We will get answers there, yes?"

* * *

The nightfall brought indigo-colored skies as the moon shone on Nicro and his army. They soared through the Adephaga, stopping at the edge of the tree truck. The steam from their breath filled the air as one D-beetle spoke, pointing down.

"They fell here my Lord, and then smashed on that tree below. They were submerged in dirt and fell from there."

Nicro stepped to the edge and looked down, glaring at his soldiers with a smirk. Then, he stepped off, plummeting down into the misty abyss. The D-Beetles all followed one by one into the unknown.

* * *

Pounding drums echo in the night sky as tri-beetles dance and chatter amongst themselves. Little beetlings' run around playing as food cooking on spits fill the air with marvelous flavors.

For what seemed like the hundredth time, Loshi noticed a few of the beetles were looking at Aniya.

"Aniya, I have a feeling you're going to have a hard time concentrating on me. It seems you have your own admirers."

Aniya nodded absently and grinned flirtatiously at some of the tribeetles. Again, she noticed the female beetles glaring at her with envy as well. She sighed.

"I feel like a meat-eater at a plant-eater party."

All the while, unbeknownst to Loshi, Teok was sneaking glances at her. A pretty female tribeetle observed this from afar. Sensing his interest was elsewhere, she ran over to Teok and kissed him on the mouth for all to see.

He recoiled quickly but before he could utter a word in protest, she pulled him out to dance.

Loshi looked on in amusement and looked at Aniya. "Well I guess you have nothing to worry about. Oh, and by the way, what's with the quick reflexes? Is there something you're hiding from me?"

Aniya had begun to answer nervously when she was interrupted by the loud sound of a gong, ending the music as all began to gather around the fire.

Loshi and Aniya were greeted and quickly taken to a section by the pit. The tribeetles all began to assemble as the old beetle sat high for all to see. Drums began to pound as tribeetles began to assemble in the center of the floor in an array of gorgeous colors, dancing to a traditional song. They moved to the thunderous beat with graceful aggression.

Teok sat with his pack and smiled as he noticed Loshi and Aniya watching the dance with wonder. The song ended as the old beetle stood and closed his eyes.

"Abato kenawando! We have unusual guests, yes?"

The tribeetles hummed and nodded.

"Our beetles are at a standstill, yes? The Gods have brought us divine intervention, yes?"

All the beetles hummed in agreement as Loshi looked at Aniya in disbelief. The old beetle looked at Loshi with a zest in his eyes. "For you to understand you must see, yes? Come, come and sit."

He pointed to the centre of the fire pit. Loshi looked around as the tribeetles stared at her, waiting to see what she would do.

She looked at the old beetle, puzzled. "You want me to sit there, in the fire?"

He nodded. "Sit, yes?"

Loshi paused for a moment in fear, but then had a strange feeling of trust in what the old beetle was telling her to do.

She cautiously stepped in as the flames began to turn to a bluish purple haze. He then put his palms out, and Loshi slowly placed her palms on his.

The ancient beetle took notice of the ring on Loshi's finger and his smile quickly faded. He looked at her with concern.

"Anikutu priass shutu?"

She looked around at the white beetles very intensely and pointed to her hand for all to see. The tribeetles looked in astonishment at the green stone. He looked deep into Loshi's eyes, then turned to the white beetles and raised Loshi's hand in the air.

"Chunto olio pacuma, Diabolo Jakiko!"

Fear seemed to wash over the tribeetles as the old beetle slid the ring off her finger and put it in the palm of her hand. He closed his eyes and put his hand over Loshi's eyes.

"Mu Sadio Kriu."

Loshi felt the ring seemingly vibrate; time began to feel like it was slowing down. Suddenly the ring began to levitate and spin in the centre of her hand. A projection of space with moving planets appeared above the ring. A beam of light flashed from one of the planets and an object streaked across to the other. Loshi's eyes lit up in awe as suddenly it hit the other planet with a loud POP. The ring's green crystal suddenly turned to a shimmering sand, leaving the ring hollow.

The old beetle put his finger in the sparkling dust and smudged Loshi's forehead.

"Pewulta Madri Shanaku." He closed Loshi's hand into a fist and covered it with his hands. He looked deep into her eyes and softly says. "Purruuuuu." Loshi blinked and suddenly she saw images of war in front of her. Raging battles and carnage, dead insects and their families around them wailing in agony, all for dominion of the stone. She began to tear up as she recognized her grandfather on the battlefield holding the ring, kneeling beside Bolas when the arrow hit his hand and the stone fell, breaking in two. Her hand began to smolder as a mysterious green skin creature walked toward Dynastis. Difficult to see through the smoke, she watched as it whispered in his ear.

"Zoondaaaa."

Loshi said it simultaneously, and it turned to her with its red fiery eyes and roared. She jolted back at this in a fright, and fell. She dropped the ring as it appeared in its true form on the ground. The tribeetles watched in amazement as the old beetle smiled at Loshi and then nodded at two beetles to help her stand.

"See, no problem." The old beetle looked at Loshi with happiness and gave her a wink. "Well, now we eat."

Loshi sat terrified, then looked at Aniya in confused silence. Aniya shrugged her shoulders and mouths the words "that was awesome." The festivities continued through the night as music and laughter echoed over the forest

* * *

Not far away, Nicro and his troops landed at the bottom of the trunk, muddy from the rain and moisture. Nicro squinted his eyes in concentration at the faint sound of white noise in the distance, and observed the dimness of a light in the dark sky miles away. Just then, a soldier tripped and landed on something with a crunch. He looked down to see chandelier pieces scattered on the ground around their feet.

"Look here my Lord, this is where they crashed."

Nicro picked up a piece of scrap and smelled it. "It's them. We will rest here until dawn. Tomorrow we search for the girl."

The D-Beetles sheltered under a bush, protecting themselves from the cool winds as they drifted off to sleep.

Nicro did not rest; he held the stone in his hand, thinking of his dead son. He gazed up at the clouds. A small opening in the sky broke wider, revealing thousands of brilliant stars. His face tightened with determination and anger, his spirit restless as he hungered for retribution.

"I will avenge you my son, you did not die for nothing. I swear to you, I will drown this forest in beetle blood." A tear ran down his cheek from his good eye. He closed it, squeezing the stone tightly.

"I promise."

Part 9

A Forgotten Past, An Uncertain Future

For the first time in the many days of somber winds and rains, the storm was over. The sky cleared and with the reemergence of the sun, the spoils of Nicro's malice were laid bare. As the water lines receded, the death toll began to climb as more and more bodies were revealed.

Nicro's army and the few who had survived were weakening from lack of food, and the damp, cold conditions. What was once a stunning empire was now a ghostly relic, like a newly excavated discovery of a historic burial ground from hundreds of years ago.

Kring entered the dining area looking unsteady and sickly, his arms shook as he gripped the chair and sat at the table. His vacant eyes were cast forward with an unemotional stare as he caught his breath. He turned slightly to look upon a beam of sunlight from the crumbled castle wall, watching the dust particles dance around and over Bruxis' dead body laying on the table.

On the other side of the long table was Queen Elytra, appearing both fearful and wary of the sight in front of her. Kring waved the guards to come closer to him.

"Nicro has left this place, gather your troops and prepare for an attack." The guard looks confused. "We have killed everyone, who will attack us?"

Kring looked up at him, stone faced. "The Mosqua from the swamps of Coridor - without Nicro, the army is vulnerable. Go quickly."

The guard nodded and exited promptly.

Across the table, a tear dropped from Elytra's cheek, splashing on the table. Kring noticed this and lowered his head, both in empathy and shame. After a moment, he spoke in a gravelly voice, "I have seen more tears than you can ever imagine. My memories are drowned in them. I have taken enough lives to make my own worthless. I'm an old beetle now, I have caused enough tears."

Queen Elytra stared down at the table, apathetic to the old beetle. Her eyes narrowed.

"Why are you telling me this? You do not have my sympathy."

He raised up his hand and turned his head, as if sheathing her anger towards him. "I do not ask for pity, nor do I deserve it. Believe it or not I was not always like this, a monster," he explained.

"I was young and full of promise once, teaching in an academic institution. I actually designed some of the early farming machines they used to build this very place…" he paused, glancing up at Elytra for a reaction.

"I was even married. To someone wonderful, my true love, but that was a long time ago…another life it seems."

Kring reached inside his cloak and retrieved a picture, glancing at it before sliding it across the table to the Queen. She picked it up and turned it over, stifling her shock in reaction to what she was looking upon. It was as if she was looking in a mirror.

"That is a picture of my Soferia."

Elytra put her hand over her mouth in disbelief.

"As you can see, you remind me of her a great deal." Kring's eyes began to tear up.

"We were so happy, but the war took everything from me, including my Soferia. My heart became black like the night sky. I lost all joy in my work; my bitterness grew and I began to build machines for monsters…"

His voice trailed off momentarily. When he glanced back at Elytra, he saw that her gaze had moved to him expectantly, so he continued.

"My machines made widows out of beetles and orphans out of children. All for nothing, all out of anger. Evil follows the stones; nothing will survive what is coming. You are free to go and find your daughter before Nicro does. If he obtains the second stone all will be lost; he is vicious and ruthless, but even he is no match for what comes for it," he paused again, as if realizing the magnitude of the words he had just spoken.

"Take my warning, outside this tree the world is unforgiving, you are not a Queen, you are prey."

Elytra slid the picture back to Kring, her anger subsiding into concern. Kring hung his head again, losing himself in the picture as she slowly exited the room, leaving him alone.

He pulled a little glass vial of the deadly venom from his cloak pocket. In the distance, he heard an eardrum-piercing screech and looked out the window to see the giant Mosqua soaring overhead. They are always ready to feed after a rainfall, and today, they are ravenous.

Kring moved to the right of the window and slid down to the ground, out of sight. With a shaking hand he raised the picture up to look upon one last time.

"My love, my love, this is goodbye. Down below I will dwell, and up above you will fly."

He uncapped the vial and drank its contents quickly, letting the reality of impending doom consume him as deeply as the poison.

* * *

The Mosqua flock descended upon the flooded city one by one, swooping and diving as they unleashed their attack on the Adephaga. The D-Beetles tried to fight them off, hacking and slicing at the airborne creatures as they stabbed and sucked, but the Mosqua were too big and powerful for their weapons. Survivors tried to escape but, they were over crowded by the blood hungry Mosqua as they thrashed through the crowds of running beetles. The children ran into hiding as the clashing of beetles and beasts spilled blood everywhere through the land, eerily reminiscent of the battle only days prior. As the attack waged on, Elytra moved quickly through the damaged palace to her bedroom and closed the door. She sat on her bed, putting her hands on Tearon's side where he usually slept, and burst into tears.

She cried heaving sobs, squeezing the sheets in her fists, burying her face into his pillow in anguish. The pain of her loss and newfound isolation washed over her once more; the grief was almost too much to bear, as were the horrors that lay outside the castle walls.

After a moment, Elytra straightened herself up, staring sullenly out the window for a moment. She wiped her tears away, composed herself and stood up, taking a few deep breaths. Her face was set with determination as she walked to the closet on the other side of the bedroom, opening the door quietly.

She reached into the back of the opening and pulled out a leather satchel. She undid its buckles and unraveled it to reveal a beautiful bow and a dozen arrows. She lifted each piece up to examine it in the light for flaws; when satisfied with their condition, she slung the sac of arrows around her shoulder and gripped the bow tightly in her hand.

The Queen took one final look around the room, feeling both calm and purposeful, and then silently slipped out of the room.

Down the corridor, a Mosqua fed on a D-Beetle loudly. She kept unnoticed as she moved stealthily down the staircase and out of the palace, jumping onto a floating door.

She used her bow to paddle herself away from the castle, quick and powerful strokes, as she anxiously looked to the horizon to welcome her away from the scene she was leaving behind. She glanced over her shoulder to see the last few D-beetles being consumed by the Mosqua, and heard the painful screams of the last dying D-Beetles fade away.

The sky began to fade to a deep indigo as night fell around Elytra. Onward she stroked. She felt that newly familiar loneliness and became nervous thinking about what Kring had told her. As the thoughts of fear and doom danced through her mind, she suddenly heard a faint whisper.

"My Queen..."

She paused her strokes, thinking of the traumatic events she had just survived and wondering if she was losing her mind. She ignored it and continued to paddle.

"My Queen..."

This time she puts the bow deep in the water to slow the door. She climbed to her feet and peered into the blades of grass and shrubs that lined the river, and squinted in the darkness.

"Who's out there? Show yourself!"

The bushes began to rattle as a little beetling's head popped up, then another and then another. Their eyes glowed faintly as they blinked repeatedly; seemingly they were in hiding.

Elytra let out a silent sigh of relief at the terrified little beetles.

"Stay here until morning, you'll be safe. I will return for you, no matter what. Stay together."

The little beetling's nodded as she began to paddle again.

"Stay together, no matter what."

She continued to move downstream, and disappeared into the mist.

* * *

Meanwhile, deep in the forest, Nicro and his four soldiers were continuing on their hunt when the burning of something woody and sweet caught their attention. They followed the scent to its source, up a tall tree and out onto its limb. The giant regal butterfly was perched up under a big leaf once again. He sat there with his legs crossed, smoking a cigar and reading a leafy newspaper. He folded his paper in half horizontally, revealing his thick mustache and fuzzy eyebrows.

"Well, well, well... more beetles! I take it you're chasing the two dames and the night light?" His cigar bobbed up and down as he spoke, his bushy brows furrowed.

Nicro's grinned broadly at this revelation, which was not unnoticed by the butterfly.

"Yes, two beetle girls, they survived a life threatening fall, and we are conducting a rescue mission. Have you seen them?"

The butterfly leaned forward and noticed him covered in insect blood. He blew a large plume of smoke at them, causing them all to cough. When the smoke cleared, he was hovering over them, carrying two puffy flowers in each arm. They were pink with silvery green spots and their anthers followed Nicro's every movement. The flowers' stigmas pulsated like a heartbeat, in anticipation.

Nicro's soldiers took out their weapons, growling and snarling, ready to attack. The butterfly's anthers quickly aim at them. He cocked both flowers and smiled.

"Make one little move and I'll squirt some seeds on ya, see? If you know what's good for ya you'll get outta here."

The beetle soldiers began to advance when suddenly, the butterfly squeezed the flowers under his arms and opened fire on the beetles.

They sprayed like an apache helicopter, obliterating stems and grass blades. The soldiers scattered and took cover behind a cluster of large mushrooms as the butterfly reloaded.

"Come on out, I got some more for ya!"

Nicro glanced at his beetles from behind the fungus, crouched to the ground, with a searing smile. He took the glowing stone from his chest-plate and slowly pushed it into his bad eye through the layers of flesh. The green glow pulsated and beams of green light began to emanate through his scar-riddled body. His troops stepped back in fear, as he grew in size.

He stood and flexed with a heavy growl, his veins became noticeably enlarged with the green glow as it was pushed to the surface from his increased muscle mass. His breath grew heavier as he clenched his fists and looked at his terrified soldiers. He opened his mouth to speak, and the sound that came out was terrifying.

"I will take this forest like I took the Adephaga! You are witness to the birth of a God."

He stepped out and faced the butterfly, who flew closer for a better look at Nicro's monstrous change in appearance.

"I'm gonna give ya one last warning see; drop the gem and scram, or else you're not like what's comin' to ya!"

Nicro moved his head from side to side, feeling the snap and crack of his neck under the strength of the stone.

"Give it your best shot."

The butterfly lowered his weapons and had a long puff from his cigar. He paused to look at it appreciatively, then ashed it on a damp leaf. He shook his head and smiled slightly.

"I warned ya..."

He flew off into the clouds as Nicro looked at his beetles with satisfaction.

Suddenly, one by one, each D-beetle was grabbed by a pink tongue and whipped up into the air. The tongues were long and sticky and wrapped tightly around each beetle with no room to move or breathe. A rhythmic humming sound could be heard and started to get closer and closer.

Nicro looked around nervously.

Tiny blue frogs begin to emerge out of the leaves with spears and harpoons aimed at him. Following behind them, dozens of tiny frogs with bows and arrows all dropped to one knee and aimed at Nicro, who was puzzled by what lay before him.

Out of the green haze, a beautifully crowned frog, vibrant and exquisite, emerged upon a gold throne carried by a giant mud green toad. They moved through the middle of the archers and stopped; two frogs stepped to each side of her, fanning her with giant lily pads as she looked at Nicro with unaffected arrogance. She leaned forward and stroked the toad, who looked equally unaffected by Nicro and his army. She looked up at the beetles dangling in the air and then looked at Nicro, blinking slowly, tilting her head to the side.

"You are not amongst friends here beetle, drop your sword."

Nicro frustratingly roared in anger. "Have you no wits, frog? You cannot kill me, I am a God!"

The Blue Frog Queen snickered and some of the other frogs followed in laughter.

"You are no God! The Jakiko do not create Gods, it is an illusion. A deception. Drop your sword or face the consequences."

Nicro stood enraged, his veins pulsating. He pointed menacingly to the Queen frog. "Let go of my beetles or else! Can't you see my power, can't you see that I can destroy you?!"

The Queen's smile faded quickly. Without warning, two D-Beetles simultaneously shot up in the air and violently smashed back down to the ground. Their bodies lay broken by the impact of their fall. Suddenly, they shot up again, smashing back down into a bloody heap. The beetle army looked on in horror, stepping back from the horrifying site of their comrades bloody demise.

Two more toads stepped out to face Nicro; he looked around at the dozens of tiny blue frogs surrounding him. The tiny Queen was lowered off her chair and she began to walk toward him, showing no fear; the toads followed behind her, watching Nicro's every move.

"There is one word we all fear in this forest. This word is never spoken, our nightmares are created by it. If you hear it, death follows. You have what it wants. It can take you at any time, even in your dreams. If these beasts regain that stone everything will be lost."

Nicro's anger began to turn to exasperation.

"I fear nothing, let whomever come and I will destroy them all!"

The green glow of the stone began to brighten quickly as a tongue came at him fast, wrapping around his leg. Nicro turned and kicked out, seeing a toad launch toward him and he quickly sliced it in half. Blood spattered as the frogs shot their arrows but they all deflected off his glowing body. That was not the case for his remaining soldiers as they were riddled by the hail of arrows ending there lives painfully slow. Nicro looked around in in realization that he was alone.

The tiny frog Queen put her hand up. "Enough!"

Nicro stood toe to toe with the blue Frog Queen. The wind gently blew as they looked at each other eye to eye, waiting for a first move. Nicro pulled back his weapon ready to strike. The warrior frogs moved in to protect their Queen, but she stopped them.

"Halt, lower your weapons at once!"

Nicro laughed eerily as he moved closer to the brave Queen. "No matter, they can't protect you, you are mine."

She closed her eyes tightly for a moment, seemingly in defeat, before suddenly opening them to reveal a glowing piercing blue light. She began to slowly levitate off the ground, as Nicro stood in awe.

"You will not kill me, beetle. You will see that I am more powerful than you can ever be, with or without the stone"

Nicro pulled back his sword, ready to swing, when suddenly the Queen raised her fist, shattering Nicro's sword. He looked at the improbable crumpled pieces in his hand and gave her a scathing stare. The little blue frog suddenly looked up at something redirecting her attention.

He turns around to see Elytra in the trees with a bow and arrow pointed right at him and before he could say a word, she let go.

The arrow directly hit the stone, impaling it through his skull to reveal a hole the size of a pinhead. Nicro collapsed to the ground dead. The stone bounced across the rocky ground, landing in front of the Frog Queen. She looked up at Queen Elytra, and grinned broadly.

Part 10

With Death Comes Hope

The sun shone on the floral huts, warming them and evoking their fragrance. The wind swiftly picked up wonderful scents and carried them through the village, which woke the tribeetles early. Once awake, they packed food and supplies onto a carriage made from intertwined twigs and leaves, skillfully sewn and designed.

Loshi and Aniya were helped into the carriage by Teok. Athara approached the carriage window and took Loshi's hand.

"You're in good hands, need not to worry. The Seers are stubborn and old, but they are divine. May the Gods watch over you." Athara earnestly smiles and turns to leave.

Loshi smiled and looked past her as she walked away to see Teok and Soura, the female beetle from the fire, speaking together. At that moment, she noticed Loshi watching them and quickly embraced Teok, as if to demonstrate her ownership of him.

The old tribeetle whistled and four potato bugs scurry to him; they curled up into little balls and rolled underneath the carriage. Athiok cracked his whips forward, striking the backs of two long golden centipedes which jolted them into action.

Moving slowly at first, they began to gain speed and pulled the carriage uphill as Teok and his best hunter Metwa followed on foot, all heading toward the Black Forest.

The village grew smaller and smaller behind them, eventually disappearing from sight. As they traveled closer to the forest, the sky began to dim and the temperature began to drop.

The old tribeetle tapped the carriage with his shaft, prompting Loshi to look out the window and then fearfully she looked back at Aniya. Teok pulled out two hatchets, and Metwa unsheathed his wasp stingers made into hand weapons. They flanked each side of the carriage and moved forward on foot as they entered the shadows.

From the tree leaves to the rugged bark, every sapling was entirely black. The grass on the ground and even the flowers and the dirt were the color of charcoal. The tribeetles' white shells and colorful markings brightly gleamed against the dimness of the landscape as they carefully navigated the trail. Aniya noticed a gooey glowing liquid dripping off some of the leaves.

"Why is everything black?" she asked curiously.

Metwa answered, "The land is a burial ground for fallen Kings. The land is forever in mourning."

Suddenly, the stone, which had been in Loshi's hand throughout the journey where it could be protected, began to vibrate and emanate its gleaming bright light through the carriage windows. The old beetle took notice and abruptly pulled back on the centipedes to halt. Teok thrust his hand into the carriage and covered Loshi's ring to hide the light.

Within seconds, long glowing green objects began to slither down the trunks of the trees, moving quicker the lower they got, as if the bark was bleeding. One by one, they gathered in formation and slowly inched toward the carriage - a ghastly vision.

The old beetle looked at Teok with concern. "We are not alone. Nuba acroba Millapedia."

Metwa stretched his arms as if preparing to fight.

The giant glowing millipedes suddenly rose from the ground, strong and lean, their spike-like legs and arms hypnotically swaying as if underwater. Slowly, a large millipede moved forward, facing the old beetle.

"Who dares to enter the forest of dead Kings? This is sacred ground, we do not take kindly to trespassers."

Loshi gripped Aniya's hand as Teok looked to her to cover the ring as he let go to grip his weapons. Athiok dropped to the ground and stepped forward in front of the millipede.

"We mean no harm, we travel in peace."

The millipede quickly responded, "To where are you all traveling, beetle?"

Teok stepped forward and answered, "To Eboulo Mountain. We seek wisdom from the Seers."

The millipede's eyes open widely in surprise. "The Seers are not expecting visitors, turn around and leave this place at once! We are at the brink of war, the Seers can't help you or anyone else."

"We come to tell them they were wrong." The millipede replied in a hostile manner.

"How dare you, the Seers are a direct link to the Gods! They are never wrong! Your blasphemy ends now."

The millipedes straightened up and began to move toward them. Aniya elbowed Loshi. "Let it shine," she whispered. Loshi uncovered the ring and bright light pierced through the carriage windows.

She slowly opened the door and stepped out, making her way towards the large millipede. His lips began to quiver and his eyes began to tear at the sight of the stone in her hand.

"Our dreams have been dark as of late, we had lost hope. Threats from over the mountain persist and we are not powerful enough to survive an onslaught."

The glow of the ring softened as Loshi stepped to him.

"War against who? I don't understand."

He moved closer to Loshi, so close that his luminosity reflected in her face. "You will speak to the Seers, your questions will be answered. Your passage will be safeguarded, you have my word stone barrier."

The millipedes turned and slowly slithered back up into the trees; she climbed back into the carriage, and onward they went.

* * *

As the pandemonium settled, Elytra climbed down from her vantage point and approached the Frog Queen. She paused, turned to the stiff body of Nicro that lay at her feet. She knelt down, retrieved an arrow from her satchel and stabbed it into the side of his engorged neck for good measure. No movement.

She wiped a tear of restrained catharsis from her eye, and noticing a drop of Nicro's blood on her hand, she quickly wiped it onto her garment as if it were poison.

The tiny Frog Queen placed her hand on Queen Elytra's arm. "You may of saved my life...thank you, brave beetle."

Elytra looked at the Frog Queen with tear-filled eyes.

"He destroyed my kingdom and killed my King, my Love. Now, I search for my daughter, who fled during the attack. That is why I am here," she paused, picked up the green stone and handed it to the frog. "This is why my kingdom is no more. Take it and do with it what you must."

The Frog Queen paused to examine the stone, then turned to face her army, raising it triumphantly in the air to the applause and jubilation of all the tiny frogs. After a moment, she turned back to Elytra.

"This is hope for all that live in this forest. I deeply feel your loss and the pain you have endured, but you are here for a purpose. This is fulfilling the prophecy. We will help you find your child, but we must take the stone to the Seers before it is too late. We are at the brink of war and we need to prepare."

Elytra was puzzled at this. "War with who? What prophecy? I have heard about this prophecy before by the beetle who killed my King. No more mysteries, please tell me what all this means."

The tiny blue frogs jumped up and moved closer, perching at the giant toads feet, followed by all the other frogs, like children in school ready to hear a story. She sat back on her thrown and began.

"It goes back a long time ago, when the Ants lost the war. As you may know, a green stone soared from the heavens and over time, it had broken into three. What you may not know of is another stone. A red stone discovered years before, which gave the Ants their ultimate strength. Two stones, a true test from the Gods," she paused for a moment, as if replaying the tale in her mind carefully before continuing.

"They say the stones are the hearts of two Rhyn Gods. The God Natha was the God of Prosperity. He was kind. He helped flourish the land for all to live. The other was Athixi, the Goddess of Greed. She was in the hearts of evil insects. She was a collector of souls and you would here her say the dreaded word "Zoonda - Mine" when she took for her collection. Natha's green stone was the bringer of life, it helped make us all what we are today. Each piece gave power, good or evil, to those who used or misused it. The red stone was the bringer of death, war and destruction and brought an evil power capable of things unimaginable. The forest was divided into two realms. The green stone landed north-east and the land flourished, as did its species. The red stone landed south-west, which devastated the forest, turning it to desert."

The tiny frog pointed to a mountain in the distance. "That is Eboulo Mountain, where we are headed to seek wisdom from the Seers. It separates the two realms," She added.

The Frog Queen nodded, and continued. "On the other side of that mountain is the sea of Duratha, which separates the land. Cross that and there is a palace within a kingdom in the center of the desert, magnificent in size. It is the home of the Pria Mantuu, the Kings of the desert. The largest and most deadly of all the insects. They conquered the Ants, and the red stone went missing for centuries. They named the desert Sada and it was ruled by two Kings, who were twin brothers. The first, King Nrobo, he was a kind and gentle Mantuu. He followed a path of goodwill, and dedicated his services to education and helping those less fortunate. His brother King Kaba was mighty and brave. He controlled the military and trade, protecting the land with deadly force for the region was rich with wondrous materials. One day, Nrobo fell in love with a poor farm girl named Kaiza. He thought she was the most beautiful in all the land. But so did Kaba. Upon learning that the love for his brother was requited, he became overwhelmed with envy. One day, after witnessing Kaiza and Nrobo kiss, Kaba's bitter jealousy bowled over and he confronted his brother. This led to a war of words, then ended in a violent conflict in which Kaba attacked and killed Nrobo. When Kaiza found Kaba drenched in blood, she panicked and feared the worst. Upon discovering her beloved Nrobo's lifeless body, she was overcome with grief. Unable to be without her true love, she ran to the edge of a nearby cliff and plunged to her death."

"Heartbreaking," Elytra interjected. "Truly. But what does this have to do with why I am here?"

"Patience, my dear," soothed the Frog Queen, "hear this and all will be revealed."

Elytra exhaled under her breath, shifted her position, and listened as the Frog Queen continued.

"As her body sank to the bottom of the sea, a brilliant red light appeared from below; as sinister and diabolical as when it led the Ants into countless wars. The red stone pulled her in instantly with its intoxicating radiance. As she sank further and further, her mind and heart still filled with pain and rage, the stone, evil in its ways, only stoked these feelings within her. It sensed her longing, her refusal to live without her beloved, and a silent covenant was made. Kaiza surrendered herself, body and spirit, for a chance to be with Nrobo again. As Kaiza committed herself to this covenant, she felt the power of the red stone within her grasp. Her eyes blazed, her skin paled, and the color drained from her face. Suddenly, her rage became tangible; a boundless energy lifting her from the depths of the dark sea, still clutching the stone in her hand. She rose from the water and confronted King Kaba for his despicable deed. He stood terrified at the dead beetle before him. Fearing for his life and seeing that Kaiza was no longer the gentle girl whom he loved, he begged for his life in exchange for giving up his kingdom. The Mantuu Queen Kaiza appeared to her people with her staff in the air and the red stone on the end, displaying her great power for all to see. She raised the staff high, the sun shining through it and casting a red hue over the Sada, reaching each of the people in the beloved land. The once-gentle and peaceful souls of these Mantuu became savage warriors. Their eyes were red as fire, their demeanors were unrecognizable and void of life. She roared the dreadful word "Zoonda" as it echoed into there minds. Kaiza still full of rage but feeling vindicated in her absolute power, knew that there was only one thing she would need to solidify her reign. She looked to Kaba, who was almost trembling in fear and shame for what he had indirectly caused, and ordered him to bring her the green stones."

A hush had fallen over the cluster of all captivated by the story. Elytra looked at the faces of all the tiny frogs, and then climbed to her feet. "Where are the Mantuu now?"

The Frog Queen, looking to the distance without breaking her gaze, responded quietly. "They are crossing the sea to begin their climb over the mountain. We must take the stone to be protected by the Seers. The only way to defeat her is if all three stones come together."

Queen Elytra's concern gave way to worry, her face suddenly contorted with fear. Her silence caught the Frog Queen's attention.

"What is it? What is so troubling?"

Elytra looked deep into her eyes. "My daughter carries another of the green stones. We must find her. I fear for her life."

The Frog Queen's brow furrowed with concern, and she agreed. "She is certainly in grave danger. These forests and woods are no place for her to be right now. We must find her, and quickly."

With that, they all determined that the course of action was set off to Eboulo Mountain together in search of Loshi and Aniya. The Frog Queen surmised that by now, if Loshi was alive, she would have been pointed in that direction by whomever she had sought help from. A small encampment of the frogs and toads were dispatched to the Adephaga to rescue any remaining survivors, bring them to safety, and await Queen Elytra's return.

Part 11

The Converging of Two Worlds

The shaking carriage rumbling over the rocky terrain and then coming to an abrupt halt awoke Loshi from a deep sleep. Confused and foggy, she rubbed the sleep from her eyes and noticed she was still surrounded by darkness. She suddenly was aware that she was alone in the carriage, and felt a surge of panic creep over her. Aniya's usual spot in the carriage was now vacant; she was nowhere to be seen.

Loshi peered out the window, seeing nothing but an unfamiliar landscape that was very dimly lit by the light of the moon. She called out Aniya's name, but there was no response. Frightened, she stepped out of the carriage slowly and walked ahead into the brush, calling out to Aniya again, and still not a sound.

Suddenly, Loshi heard a soft whisper, as if it were blowing through the trees like a breeze.

"Do not fear, come to me."

She moved forward bravely, yet cautiously, following the haunting voice. "Hello, who's there? Show yourself."

A faint glow emanated from the blades of grass behind a gated patch of land adorned with vines; this drew Loshi's attention as she entered past the gates and into a clearing. Her eyes scanned the area she had stumbled upon. It appeared to be an ancient burial ground. Low lying stone graves spread out as far as her eyes could see, old and weathered from the elements of many years past.

She walked curiously amongst the stones, through the blackness, and came to the massive mausoleum of an Ant King from long ago. It had decayed through time and broken pieces of the structure were scattered on the ground around it, mixed with the black leaves and flowers.

The scent of licorice and moss filled her senses. She knelt down and touched one of the black flowers, and it immediately turned to a bright pink and then faded into a deep purple. Mystified, she dragged her hand across the flower bed and they all morphed from blacks to blues, from whites to oranges.

Her ring began to pulsate as she heard a sound from inside the tomb. She stepped closer to the mouth of the tomb to investigate.

"Hello?"

All of the sudden, the walls of the monument began to shake. Dust began to seep out of the opening in a large plume. The sound of creaking and shifting within caused Loshi to fearfully step back. A ghastly figure stepped out from the crypt, dragging its limbs, clattering with every step. His body was brittle and decomposed, a truly startling sight. Loshi realized she was looking at the corpse of the Ant King.

She stepped back nervously, terrified, losing her footing and stumbling as the Ant King lurched closer towards her. His crown, dusty and imposing on his frail skull, shook with every movement. He stopped within inches of Loshi's face so that she could feel the coldness coming off of his bones.

"Beware, keeper of the stone... beware, for death comes for you...heed my words, unless the stones are made whole, you will turn to dust."

He leaned closer and his sunken eye sockets lit up under the glow of the ring, illuminating his translucent facade.

"It comes for you, beware, the red stone comes for you. You must seek the other stones, or you will perish!"

With that, Loshi awoke with a start as the carriage came to an abrupt stop. She glanced frantically to her left, then let out a sigh of relief when she saw that Aniya was there.

Teok approached the carriage door and opened it, holding out his hand to help the girls out. "This is as far as the carriage goes. We must walk from here."

Aniya gave Loshi a concerned look, then noticed Loshi's bewildered expression.

"What's wrong? Are you ok?"

Loshi looked at her with dismay. "I had another dream, and it was troubling."

They stepped out of the carriage, and gazed up at the mountain. Athiok walked ahead of them and used his shaft to bend the blades of grass in an effort to make a trail for them to follow. Teok and Metwa brought up the rear of the group, aware and alert of their new surroundings. They stopped at the base of the mountain; Athiok tapped his shaft on the limestone that rippled through the base.

"We are here, yes?"

Teok and Metwa nodded and began gathering belongings. Loshi and Aniya stared up at the gigantic rock, bending almost backward as they attempted to get a view of the top.

"How are we getting up there?" Aniya asked apprehensively.

Athiok grinned mischievously. "Oh, you will see."

He tapped the stone again in a rhythm, which made a humming sound as the shaft vibrated. He waved his shaft around, making the humming stronger. The sound of wings flapping and threshing got stronger and stronger. Just then, a beautiful dragonfly soared down from the top of the peak in a smooth figure eight. It landed in a graceful and dramatic stance, proud like a peacock. It was stunning in its turquoise and yellow feathers, its wings were like four crystal leaves, shining and radiant. The magnificent insect lowered its wings down like a ramp, cueing the travelers to come aboard.

The sound of something clearing its throat came from the head of the dragonfly, where a small flea was perched. He then spoke into a long birch leaf which was fashioned into a conical speaking aid, allowing the passenger to hear his otherwise tiny voice.

"Good Morning, beetles! Welcome aboard this flight to the **Top of the Mountain!** My name is Sork and I'll be your In-flight Service Director & Captain for your journey today. I'm here to ensure you have a safe and enjoyable flight, so please fasten your seat belts and prepare for takeoff."

The dragonfly's wings began to beat, starting off slow and picking up speed, then taking off into the clouds. The passengers barely had enough time to prepare themselves for the sharp vaulting into the air, which caught them off guard, but were soon overcome with the captivating view of the land below.

"Good Morning again beetles, this is your Captain speaking. We are currently cruising at an altitude of 1.2 feet and are ascending at an airspeed of 52 miles per hour. Judging from the angle of the sun, the time is early morning. The current weather conditions for our flight are calm and favorable, and with the tailwind on our side we are expecting to land on **Top of the Mountain** ahead of schedule. The weather on **Top of the Mountain** is clear and sunny, with a low of really really cold, and windy... and...well, it's freezing actually. I'll talk to you again before we reach our destination. Until then, sit back, relax and enjoy the rest of the flight to the **Top of the Mountain.**"

They soared through the skies, weaving higher and higher as the trees and grounds below them became smaller and smaller. For the first time in their lives they could see all the forests in all their beauty. Never-ending pastures, treetops and waterfalls surrounding the Black Forest below them. As they ascended higher and higher, Loshi could see the tree trunk in the distance that was once their home. It shrank into a small speck on the horizon as they approached the higher plateaus of the mountain until what was once their home was gone.

Teok and Loshi sat across from each other, intermittently glancing at each other shyly and then looking away. Aniya noticed this and gave Loshi a look, as if to say "What are you waiting for?!"

Unsure of how to open a conversation, Loshi took notice of a scar on Teok's right shoulder. "Umm...quite the wound. How did it happen?"

Teok touched it instinctively, and looked at her. "I got this when I was a child. The elders had heard that the ants were going to invade our village, so my father hid us up in the hills. But one night, they came when we slept. We tried to run, but there were so many of them. My sister and my mother and I thought we were close to safety when an arrow grazed me and hit my mother. It killed her and my siblings inside her. The village is all that is left of our beetles."

Loshi was silent, and looked down at her ring sadly. "Do you have anything to remind you of her?" she asked softly.

"Sadly, no. This scar is my only reminder. We were very young, so I sometimes struggle to remember her face. I worry one day I won't be able to." Teok stared at the horizon, expressionless.

Loshi looked up at him, glossy-eyed. Suddenly, some rocky turbulence threw her off her seat and into his arms. Their faces were close, so close they could almost -

"This is your Captain speaking! Apologies for that little bumpy ride there, but passengers need not worry as it should be smooth flying from here on out."

They looked at each other sheepishly and smiled; Loshi sat back down in her seat. She glanced at Aniya for a millisecond, whose eyes and mouth were open with surprise.

Loshi and Teok continued their conversations, learning of each other's past and their lives up until then. Aniya filled Athiok and Metwa in on escaping with the stone, and being hunted by Nicro and his killer beetles. Both of them listened intently as she recounted the events with vivid enthusiasm. They were all so deep in conversation that they were unaware of the great heights they were soaring to. Teok looked down, motioning for Loshi to do the same. She couldn't believe the ground had disappeared. All there was below them now were clouds - beautiful, fluffy and captivating.

The Captain's voice came through again. "We have just been cleared to land on **Top of the Mountain!** We hope you had a pleasant flight and a wonderful experience flying with us today. Take care, and safe travels."

The dragonfly reached the peak and slowly ascended to the ground. The clouds began to blow away from his massive thrashing wings as the stoney ground rushed to meet them.

* * *

On the other side of the mountain, hundreds of boats cut through the cresting waves, sweeping steadfast through the water towards their destination. Kaiza and her Mantuu army were sailing to the mountain. The harsh winds and salty spray stung the rowers' faces as they stroked strongly and in fierce unison.

In her bedchamber, Kaiza eyes opened suddenly as she awoke from a deep sleep. Even though they were days away, she could feel the power of the green stones. She ran her fingers across the tomb of her dead love, Nrobo.

"Sleep now, my love; for you will awaken once again."

She exited her bedchamber, and stepped to the edge of the ship. Her eyes became red reminiscent of Athixi the Dark Goddess. She opened her mouth and three tiny red moths flew out one by one, shaking and flapping their wings. She whispered three ancient words to them, filling them with spoken venom, and they flew off into the clouds above and towards the mountain.

Part 12

Death From Above

The peak of the mountain was cold and windy. Tiny snow crystals fluttered in the air like little diamonds sparkling in the sun. The terrain was surrounded by a dazzling array of icicles spiking upwards through the ground as if they were shooting out of the earth. The sun shone brightly through the ice formations, creating a crystal cascade of colors reflecting off each other. The land was visibly wind-worn as seen by the pockets of grass scattering the rocky tundra, pulled out of their roots.

They all followed the ice path leading up to a free standing earthy green door at the cliff of the mountain. It was not like the nut and stem-made doors that they were accustomed to; it was like nothing they had ever seen before. Adorned in great ornate detail and it seemed to be...alive.

The vines grew from out of the ground and slowly moved up the door like a living organism, ebbing and flowing in a rhythmic state throughout its shape. They stepped closer to this curious door, shivering from the cold. Athiok looked back at all of their intrigued faces, and smiled. He put his hand on the door knob and slowly turned it, pushing the door open to reveal bright rays of sunshine on the other side, with nothing below their feet but air. He stepped through to the other side.

"WAIT!!" Loshi yelped in shock. She peered over the edge of the cliff frantically to see if he fell over, but he was not there.

She looked at the others, bewildered, and cautiously put her arm through the door. Aniya stepped to the side of the door, and was alarmed to see it did not show on the other side. She and Aniya looked at each other in amazement, speechless at this discovery.

Metwa shook his head and smiled; he walked through immediately, seemingly disappearing into thin air.

Loshi couldn't believe her eyes. "Where did they go? What's going on?"

Teok extended his hand out to Loshi. "Trust me, this is beyond logic or reason. You'll just have to take the first step and see."

She took his hand, as well as Aniya's, and they followed him through the mysterious door, to the other side.

* * *

Once beyond the door, they followed Athiok into a warm, Eden-like place - a stark difference from the snowy landscape they had just left behind. This place was ripe with luscious green plants and trees filled with an abundance of exotic flowers and fruits. Through the beautiful garden, the soil was rich and full of life with all sorts of growing wonders. They were surrounded by the most beautiful plants that burst with pinks and blues, and intoxicating scents that dazzled the senses. The wind blew softly, spreading fluffy pollen crystals through the air.

They came to a stone platform and in the centre were three circles, one beside each other, filled with soil that had carvings etched around the edges. They looked as if they were placed to protect and guard the beautiful elaborately designed ovular nest behind them. The nest was made from vines and plant stems intertwined within itself creating a perfect shape. The inside of the nest glowed green with the piece of a Jakiko stone placed at the centre, which was seemingly palpitating.

A small ramp guided them to the stone. Loshi cautiously stepped up to the platform. She had barely taken two steps when simultaneously both stones burst in a flash, the force pushing her back so hard that she stumbled. Teok grabbed her arm to steady her back onto her feet.

The soil in the three circles began to shake; lightly at first, and then trembling quite obviously. The dirt began to bubble and swirl as three giant earthworms slowly rose from the soil. The carvings around the rings began to shimmer as their golden brown wrinkly bodies slithered out with dirt sticking to their slimy skin. Their eyes were a piercing blue that sparkled like two sapphires. They slowly turned their heads one by one, looking directly at their visitors, and beginning to softly speak in rhyme.

"We are the Seers, the oracles of the Gods, the tellers of future years. The words birthed in antiquity have now come to be, the prophecy is death, the end of you and me."

Athiok gently moved closer, resting his staff down. "Wise oracles, we have come to bring you hope in these troubled times." He gestured for Loshi to come forward and show them the ring on her hand. The earthworms recoiled slightly, taken aback at what was being presented before them.

"How can this be? We did not foresee. Could there be hope against the evil sailing the sea?"

The Seers leaned in close to Loshi with graveness in their eyes.

"Evil comes with a storm at her tail, find the third stone, lest your time grow stale. Take this protected stone and leave, for in three days, there will be much to grieve."

Loshi stands pleadingly with confusion in her voice. "Why me? I am just a girl, I am no warrior. The fate of the world can't depend on me."

"We did not question what the Gods chose to be, we only see what they choose us to see. You are the bringer of hope in a future of calamity, fate has brought you to fight because of tragedy. A warrior you were meant to be"

Loshi stepped back as their words sunk in deeply, thinking about the events that led her to this point. Just then, in his periphery, Metwa noticed three red moths flying towards them. He squinted at them suspiciously, and elbowed Teok to alert his attention to them. Aniya noticed as well, but far more naively. They fluttered around her head, and she giggled.

"Look how cute these little guys are!" she exclaimed.

Suddenly, Athiok's face hardened and he whirled around to face Metwa. "Abaroatu sota kobo, sata!"

Metwa nodded quickly. "He senses an evil presence, we must leave at once."

The three little moths flitted about for a few more seconds, then darted over to the Seers. Before the earthworms could react, the moths whispered their toxic message into their ears. Instantly, they dropped to the ground, their wrinkly bodies wriggling in struggle.

Athiok looked at Metwa and Teok. "We have big trouble, yes?"

The Seers' eyes changed from a crystal blue sparkle to a fluorescent purple. From the ground, all three earthworms craned their heads to look at the beetles.

"Evil is here! If you want to survive, take the stone and run, run, run for your lives!"

All the sudden, the Seers' eyes went from purple to a fiery red. Smoke seeped from the corners of their mouths. Their faces, once exuding peace and calm, twisted and contorted to a glower, as if they were possessed by the words spoken by the moths. They stared down Metwa and Teok as they slowly rose up from their prone position on the ground, to a position of attack. Before the beetles could react, the earthworms opened their mouths and let out a menacing roar that shook the ground.

Loshi and Aniya, horrified by what was transpiring before them, ran to Athiok for safety. He grabbed both their hands.

"This is no time to panic. We must find shelter quickly, follow me!"

They ran to the trees, skittering up the trunk and disappearing into the leaves.

Metwa and Teok turned to face the worms bravely as they slowly slithered toward them. Their saliva dripped from their mouth openings, singeing the earth as it fell, igniting the ground below them in a destructive trail of fire.

"You will see, Doom comes for thee!"

Athiok ran across a branch just over Metwa and Teok; he looked down at his brave son and closed his eyes. The end of his staff ignited in a brilliant white light; he took a piece of a tree leaf, and touched it with the bright light.

"Baruku Atwatu Meko..."

His staff flashed and the leaf became hard like a shield. He alerted the beetles' attention and dropped the shield into Teok's hand, who then threw it to Metwa. Athiok hastily created another with his staff and dropped it down.

Using his shield as cover, Metwa pulled one of his stingers and threw it at the Seers, puncturing the middle worm in its side. The worm shrieked in agony, fire oozing from its mouth, causing the other two worms to look in anger at the causer of their comrades' pain. They breathed in deeply, and exhaled three massive fire balls at Metwa, exploding onto his shield and throwing both beetles back into a bush.

The Seer's blood was evidently as fiery as its saliva; as blood poured out of its wound, it scorched its side and derma, making him roar in pain. Teok ran to Metwa, pulling him deeper into the bush and out of the Seers' sights. He patted the fire out aggressively and looked up at Athiok in both exasperation and relief, letting him know they were ok.

The old beetles began to climb the tree further up and Aniya looked at Loshi with a notion.

"They need my help - you move carefully and grab the stone. I will help them."

Loshi's eyes widened. "You are not a warrior, you'll get hurt!"

Aniya's face was set with determination. "Don't worry about me, I can handle myself. Go quickly, and be careful!"

Aniya proceeded to climb up, following Athiok.

Loshi hesitated for a second, took a deep breath, cautiously started toward the nest. Metwa glanced over at Teok as he shook the cobwebs from his head, then resting his head in his hands with a look of hopelessness.

"Our weapons are useless. We need a plan."

Overhead, Athiok extended his hand to Aniya and helped her to the top of the tree. They looked on nervously as Loshi snuck to the bottom of the nest, unseen. Aniya turned to Athiok, shaking her head.

"We need to keep their attention from Loshi, otherwise she will surely be spotted. Here, I can help..."

She pressed on her shiny flat earrings, and her body was immediately enveloped in the uniform of her shadow ninja attire, revealing only her eyes. Athiok looked at her and grinned broadly. "Oh boyba, I knew there was something about you."

She smiled back with a wildness in her eyes, and in an instant, she had leaped off the tree, landing on her feet in front of the Seers. She revealed her rose thorned hand claws, ready to fight.

Behind the bush, Metwa saw the young Aniya drop to the ground in front of them, standing bravely, and alerted Teok. They were pleasantly taken aback at the sudden brazenness of the young shadow ninja and emerged from the bush, flanking her on each side in solidarity.

The Seers, seemingly undeterred, slinked menacingly towards the beetles, fire still dripping from their mouths. Suddenly, one of the earthworms let out a low moan, cocked its head back, and spewed a powerful surge of fire into the bush over the beetles' shoulder. The second and third earthworm followed suit, igniting an inferno around them. Tree trunks flickered and then smoldered, blackening the sky with smoke.

Aniya pulled two small axes from her belt, readying herself for battle. The earthworms saw this action, focused their piercing gaze on Aniya and sped toward her.

One Seer blew a blazing fireball which flew past her. Aniya tucked out of the way, bobbing deftly beneath its reach before popping up beside the middle Seer; she sliced its neck with both axes, opening its throat and spilling the fiery blood everywhere.

All the sudden, debris fell from the sky and landed on the ground in front of them. The Seer on the left craned his neck upwards to see the source; Loshi had been spotted. In her efforts to reach the stone, she had accidentally shaken twigs and mud that was caked on the branch she was crossing.

The creature wasted no time; it breathed an arc of fire at Loshi, soaring through the air like a rainbow of flames, aiming straight for her. Aniya, quick as a cricket, jumped to the bottom branch and swung her way to the nest, tackling Loshi out of the way and out of the tree, hitting the ground with a thud. The fireball hit the branch, destroying it and rapidly spreading to the other limbs as the flames from the trunk rose higher.

Aniya pulled Loshi to her feet. Both were disoriented from the impact of the fall, as well as the thick smoke that clouded their line of sight. They paused for a moment, looking around frantically for their comrades and also for the earthworms hunting them. They crouched low to the ground, using the haze to their advantage, trying to evade detection, before finally spotting Metwa and Teok huddled in a pile of twigs and running to it for cover.

It took a moment for the four of them to digest the happenings. Somehow they were still alive, but for how much longer? Their bodies were blackened from the soot, their eyes were red and watery, their limbs ached and burned. Aniya, noticing a puddle of blood on the ground underneath Loshi, tore a piece of cloth from her pant leg and wrapped it tightly around Loshi's left arm. Aniya compressed the bleeding gash, causing Loshi to wince in pain sharply.

"Are you ok? Are you hurt anywhere else?"

Loshi just stared at Aniya blankly, in shock, making Aniya squirm slightly.

"You're a…a shadow beetle? All this time"

Aniya nodded quickly, a half smile on her face. "Well of course, Princess. I DO have to be able to protect you."

Loshi smiled, shaking her head in disbelief. "That is so cool!"

Aniya squinted up her nose. "I know, right?"

Teok looked at them sternly. "We must leave now. They are too powerful and the fire is spreading. If that doorway to the other side burns, we are stuck here forever. Where is Father?"

Aniya pointed towards the treetop that she had been up in with Athiok. Seeing Aniya point up to him and the fire rising higher and higher, Athiok flung back his hooded shawl and lifted his ear to the air. He focused his gaze, hearing something from above, and looking up he spotted an enormous bird's nest up high. Using all his limbs, he skittered and climbed to the giant nest to investigate if its dwellers might be of any aid. Once he reached the nest, he glanced over the opening to see a group of oversized hatchlings sound asleep and nestled into each other, somehow oblivious to the combat waging on below them. Athiok began to shake the branch that cradled the nest. Within seconds of this turbulence, the hatchlings began to chirp loudly as they were jarred awake by their shaking hearth. The chirping of the massive, irritated chicks grew louder and louder, until it became a high pitched squawk that echoed through the landscape, startling the Seers.

Just then, Loshi stood up and stretched out her arms; the sword appeared, glowing brightly as she gripped it with both hands. The two remaining Seers roared in anger at the tenacity of the young princess.

Loshi turned to them, ready for what was to come, when suddenly she heard a high pitched noise coming from the treetops.

"What is that!?" She cringed at the sound, not wanting to show weakness but unable to shield her ears. Aniya approached, and paused pensively. "I hear it too."

Teok looked up at the white glow in the trees to see Athiok standing triumphantly on a branch, beside a giant nest. The Seers, although visibly agitated by the sound, were focused and thirsty for blood. They refocused menacingly, faces twisted in blind rage, ready to attack and kill as the beetles moved forward in unison, shielded and strong. The Seers' pace quickened as they wriggled towards the beetles, swifter than a snake slither. They arched their backs, gathering what was sure to be an explosive arsenal of fire to be unleashed.

Just then, the high pitched squawk sounded again, deafening this time, and two gigantic birds swooped towards the earth, grabbing the worms with their talons. They reared their heads back, opening their beaks wide, and finally bringing them down upon the Seers, severing each worm in half. The oversized birds pecked and fed upon the worms, reducing them to a simmering mess of ember and gore. They tossed, chewed, and swallowed until the very last morsels of the Seers were gone.

The larger bird burped a plume of smoke as the other one patted his back with his wing. "Too hot for ya, Karl?" The smaller bird squawked with laughter as he bounded across the smokey landscape, flapping his wings and heading back up to the nest to feed their young. Karl followed close behind him, smoke still seeping from his beak as he took flight.

* * *

Aniya followed Loshi to the nest that housed the stone, climbing up and then pulling Loshi to safety. Somehow, even though the nest was smoldering, the stone appeared to be perfectly intact.

As Loshi drew closer, her ring began to pulsate. The green glow appeared, and then began to emanate from her hands, her eyes. Within seconds, the green light completely covered her entire body. She felt a strange sensation coursing through her veins as she let go of the branch and began to levitate.

The two stones drew parallel to each other. The stone in the nest shook fervently until it popped out and floated up. The two stones began to merge as if there was an invisible magnet pulling them together in a tremendous beam of light. The stones swirled around each other, faster and faster until they melded as one in a small flurry of sparks.

Loshi landed back down softly on the ground, still radiating, as each beetle came closer to marvel at her magnificence. To her amazement, her armor began to fuse onto her body; a solid gold cuirass covered her back and chest, adorned with intricately carved symbols. Then, greaves for her limbs and a beautiful chalcidian style helmet that gleamed in the light.

Loshi didn't move for a moment as she allowed this metamorphosis to sink in. She was the same girl yet somehow forever transformed. She stepped to Aniya, armor shining brilliantly, and embraced her.

The group reunited in the wake of the destruction and subsequent transfiguration that they just witnessed. So much had happened, so many questions and few answers. All was silent as they made their way back through the landscape, back towards the door that gave them passage to this otherworldly place.

When they reached the peak on the mountain, Loshi looked back at the burnt out terrain. What would she be returning to? What was she returning as?

How could she possibly explain what had happened, if there was anyone left on the other side to explain it to?

Athiok took the first step through, followed by Metwa and Teok. Aniya wrapped herself in a few leaves as she walked through the door, unexcited about the cold. Loshi approached the doorway and paused; she took a final look at what they were leaving behind, then stepped through and closed the door behind her.

Part 13

The Magic and the Mayhem

As the dust was settling amidst the eerie calm, the three little moths lay still on the ground. One of the moths began to move its wings; slowly at first, and then a flutter. Within seconds, the other moths began to stir as well, gradually coming back to life and shaking off the remnants of the chaos that had just ensued.

They rose up into the air, low at first and then propelled themselves up into the sky in a circular motion, faster and faster, creating a smokey red mist in their wake.

As the red mist spread into the atmosphere around them, it faded to a morbid black and began to part in two. From the center of the billowy mist emerged a robust Kaiza, apparently rejuvenated by the devastation around her.

The moths slowed down but continued to fly above her as her feet hit the earth. She made her way purposefully to the charred triangle where the Seers once dwelled. She touched the empty spot where the stone rested, staring at it pensively before lightly flicking it, causing it to burst into tiny pieces.

Kaiza surveyed the area around her feet absently, before noticing a small puddle nearby. She knelt down beside it, looking closer at the deep yellowish green substance that had fallen from Loshi's open wound.

"Well, now...what do we have here?"

She dipped her finger into the blood and touched it to the tip of her tongue. Immediately, her aura flickered to a brighter red. Her pupils dilated and turned black and she slipped into a trance-like state.

Her mind was flooded with images of the past as she traveled through Loshi's blood-line, going back through the many years of peace and war, feast and famine, before arriving at the battleground where Dynastis had killed Bolas.

Kaiza glanced around the landscape, which was destroyed to the point of being uninhabitable. She walked through the war torn fields, maneuvering the damage and the dead and dying bodies strewn about. She stopped and crouched down next to the body of a dead beetle soldier. Seeing that he was still clutching his bow and arrow in his stiffened hands, she grabbed and pulled it from his clutches with great forces, snapping his fingers in the process.

The wind began to pick up and kicked up the dust around her. Just then, she saw Dynastis in the distance crouched low to the ground. On his finger, Kaiza saw the green glow of the ring. She planted both her feet firmly, placed the arrow and raised up the bow, pulling back slowly with its point aimed directly at Dynastis's hand.

She released without a beat and the arrow flew through the air, piercing the hand of Dynastis in a swift act. He jolted in reaction to this, then quickly scanned his surroundings, struggling to see through the dust which made it impossible to see anything more than three feet in front of him.

Out of the thick air stepped Kaiza. She approached Dynastis who lay on the ground in pain, and pressed her foot down upon his head as he gritted his teeth. The more he tried to resist with all his might, the harder she pressed him into the dirt, standing firm while she reached down to pick up half of the glowing stone.

A world away, Loshi felt a sudden chill run through her body, hitting her like a wave.

She reacted viscerally, and Aniya looked at her with concern.

"What's wrong?"

Loshi said nothing, just turned her head and grimaced.

"Loshi, what is it?"

"I - I don't know...I feel strange. Like there's something around me..."

The stones began to vibrate and loosen, and Loshi's body started to seize up. Her muscles and limbs were seemingly locked in paralysis. Aniya gasped at the sight of this and grabbed Loshi tightly, trying to shake her back into consciousness.

"Loshi! Tell me what's wrong, you're scaring me!"

Loshi's eyes rolled back and turned completely black as the vision of Kaiza on top of Dynastis with the ring in her hand played out before her.

Athiok rushed over to Loshi, whose body had now begun shaking, and put his hands on her shoulders, looking deep into her eyes.

"Araboku Mika!"

Immediately, he saw the vision of Kaiza and Dynastis that had paralyzed Loshi. The evil Mantuu reacted to his call and snapped to attention; she looked directly at him.

"Zoondaaaaa."

In her hand was the stone, and at that, she disappeared.

The second stone vanished instantaneously, right before Athiok's eyes. Loshi's body then went limp and she collapsed to the ground. Her armor disappeared, and her eyes refocused. She moaned in discomfort, in confusion.

Kaizas' eyes refocused and she returned to consciousness. She looked at the remnants of Loshi's blood on her finger, and spat out what she still had on her tongue in disgust. She held the stone to her chest in gratification and gripped it tight, embracing its strength and all that would come with it. Then, she took a deep breath, and began the short walk to the door on the mountain peak.

* * *

As the beetles helped Loshi to her feet, Athiok stopped and looked back towards the door on the mountain path; an ominous feeling crept into his consciousness.

Teok saw the unsettling look on his father's face. "What is it, Baba?"

Athiok didn't break his gaze towards the mountain. "You must go and keep the others safe. My work here is not yet done."

Teok started to protest but stopped himself, knowing that Athiok was firm in his purpose, whatever the reasoning might be. Reluctantly, he turned away and grabbed Loshi's hand and the two ran towards the dragonfly awaiting them. Metwa and Aniya followed close behind them.

Seeing that the beetles were leaving, Athiok turned his focus to the door at the top of the peak. He walked towards it, climbing higher and higher, closer and closer. As he approached the door, his staff brightened and he retrieved his sword from his cloak.

On the other side of the door, Kaiza stood staring at it, fixated. She waved her hand and gestured sharply towards the door, smashing it into pieces, scattering vines and debris everywhere. She faded into a misty red smoke and seeped through to the other side of the realm.

Athiok readied himself as the red mist took shape in front of him and formed a towering figure. Kaiza glared down at him menacingly.

"Bring me the girl and I will have mercy on your kind. Defy me, and you will suffer!"

"You cannot have her! Go back to where you dwell!"

"I am not merciful, old beetle. Give me the stone or die!" The sorceress screeched.

Athiok said nothing in response, not even flinching in the face of the evil figure before him.

"Very well, beetle...you will perish under my power." She cackled as she took the green stone and swallowed it, appalling Athiok.

She began to smolder and smoke, her eyes turned to a bright yellow. Scales protruded from her limbs and her body slowly morphed into a large red and green snake, which looked more like a dragon at three times Athiok's size. Her mouth curled into a wicked grin, her lips parted to reveal a sharp dagger-like tongue.

"Thisss isss your lassst warning, beetle. Bring me the girl and the ssstone, or I will end you."

"You shall not have it!" He raised his staff high and slammed it to the ground, which sparked and blasted a bright light in her eyes.

Athiok noticed the dragonfly carrying the beetles on its back in his periphery hovering nearby, having still not left for safety. Teok watched in horror at his father standing toe to toe with the reptilious monster.

"GO!" yelled Athiok vehemently.

Just then, the giant snake swooped down and wrapped her body around him, lifting him off the ground and squeezing him tight. He cried out in agony as the beetles all looked on helplessly, tearfully.

The dragonfly readied for takeoff, waiting for the word to leave. Athiok dropped his staff and it shattered into pieces on the ground. Kaiza laughed a low, throaty cackle, lifting him off the ground in her coils so that he was eye to eye with her.

"All will sssuffer, all will fall once the ssstones are mine."

She tightened her grip on Athiok, causing his old limbs to snap and break under the pressure. He yelped in agony. With the last bit of energy left, he looked the serpent dead in her eyes.

"She...will defeat you." He gasped for air, barely choking the words out and then pulled back his sword to slice her. He barely got his sword high enough when Zoonda opened her fang riddled jaws and brought them down over Athiok, devouring him with one bite.

"NO! NO!!" Teok yelled out in anguish, and at that, Metwa signaled the dragonfly to take off. Its giant wings began to move slowly, gaining power. Aniya wept quietly with her head in her hands. Loshi stared straight ahead, numb and expressionless in light of the sacrifice that was just made in order to protect her life. Teok glowered at the snake with malice.

All of a sudden, the serpents' glee changed to confusion, then pain. Her scaly stomach split open abruptly, spilling its contents out onto the ground, including Athiok, still gripping his sword in hand. The serpent dropped like a fallen tree in a smoky haze. No sooner did it hit the ground then Kaiza appeared from the ashes in her Mantuu form once again.

Teok broke out from Metwa's grip and leapt off the dragonfly's back, running to his father's aid. Kaiza approached the battered old beetle, grabbed his head and looked at Teok with a wry grin.

"Take one more step and you will have to answer for your precious father's death."

Teok stopped in his tracks, laid down his sword and raised his hands up in surrender. She swiped Athiok's sword off the ground and rested the tip of the blade on his forehead, piercing it enough for blood to trickle down his face. She held up the piece of the stone in her possession. It pulsated vibrantly.

"Bring me the other stone, and I will ease his suffering."

Teok trembled in anger. He said nothing in response, paralyzed in his evaluation of what he was being forced to choose between.

"Look at him, his body is broken. He is dying! I can show him the mercy he is begging for. Don't you love your father enough to end his pain?"

Teok looked back at Loshi knowing he could not give in to this evil sorceress. He also could not forsake his beloved father, who had acted so bravely to save them all.

She pushed the sword down slightly, causing Athiok to wince in pain. She then raised the sword up over his head, insinuating that her next move would end Athiok's life.

"This is your final chance, beetle."

Teok falls to his knees, accepting his father's fate. Kaiza looked visibly agitated at this, but her frustration soon turned to flippancy.

"Very well."

She raised the sword high and just as she was about to strike down, another dragonfly emerged in the light of the dawn over the peak of the mountain. Elytra

LOSHI AND THE BATTLE FOR THE GOD STONES

stood tall on the back of the dragonfly with the little blue Frog Queen floating above. The Frog Queen pointed to the circling moths that hovered above Kaiza; Elytra raised up the bow with three arrows aimed at the three red moths. Before Kaiza could understand what was about to happen, Elytra released.

"No..." the sorceress whispered sharply.

In an instant, all three arrows struck each of the three moths, making her disappear into thin air. The sword fell to the earth, landing just inches from Athiok's head. The green stone landed softly upon his chest. Teok quickly ran to his father, embracing him with tears of joy and relief.

Loshi stood staring at the two Queens atop the dragonfly, her mouth agape, not trusting her eyes that recognized her beloved mother descending towards her. She ran full speed toward Elytra, who leapt from one dragonfly to the other, and then to the ground. They embraced each other tightly, Loshi buried her face in Elytra's shoulder, her shoulders shook as she wept. Queen Elytra comforted her, stroking her head affectionately, stoic yet emotional and relieved to have reunited safely with her daughter.

Aniya and Metwa, realizing that they were holding hands, smiled at each other sheepishly. "Screw it!" said Aniya, as she yanked him in by his armor for a kiss.

* * *

Unbeknownst to the reuniting beetles, Kaiza had appeared back on her boat amongst her Mantuu army. She looked down at her empty hands and collapsed to her knees. Resting her hands on Nrobo's tomb, she let out a roar so angry that it startled the Mantuu as they rowed in unison through the crashing waves.

She walked over to the stern of the boat and gazed into the water. Tears streamed down her face, red like blood, dripping into the water. As her tears hit the currents, dead fish bobbed up to the surface. First a few, then tens, then hundreds, some the size of sharks, floating up dead to the surface, knocking the boats from side to side.

She stared straight ahead, unphased and unfettered, and then fixed her gaze upon the mountain, the beetles and the stones she left behind. She shook her head slowly, and smiled through her poisonous tears.

"You think this is over. It has only just begun."

Part 14

The Behest of the Brokenhearted

Back at the village, Athara carefully wiped the dirt and blood from Athiok's limbs as he lay resting, trying to recover from his injuries. A piece of the green stone rested upon his forehead and radiated a green glow throughout his skeleton in an attempt to heal his broken body. Athara smiled faintly as she listened to the Adephagan and tribeetle children laughing and playing together outside, sounding like cheerful music in the air.

Elytra entered the floral hut quietly and tapped on the frame, not wanting to disturb. She was greeted by Athara's welcoming voice.

"Please come in! How is your morning? I trust you slept well?"

"My morning has been pleasant, thank you. And yes, I don't think I have slept that well in quite some time."

Athara grinned knowingly and nodded. "You and your beetles have been through a great deal. We are similar in that way. I cannot thank you enough for what you did, you saved him. We are all forever grateful, we are lost without him..." her voice trailed off.

Just then, Athiok began to mutter slightly, and his eyes fluttered open. "Druba, I'm not dead yet." He reached his hand out shakily towards Elytra and she accepted it graciously. He patted the top of her head with his other hand in an act of seemingly paternal affection that made Elytra well up.

"Now now, no need for sadness, yes?"

She shook her head and smiled through her tears. "It is I who should be thanking you. You saved Loshi and Aniya, your village took them in when they had nowhere to go. I am forever in your debt."

He waved away her remark and looked at her with deep gravity. "What of your home, were there many survivors?" Elytra shook her head. "Very few lived. We lost everything, almost everyone. Homes were either destroyed or swept away. Thank the Gods that some of the children are safe, but most of them have lost their families."

Athara put her hand on Elytra's shoulder in an attempt to comfort the Queen as she sat in her mixed emotions. "You have a home here now."

"Your home is exquisite! I have never seen such flowers, such colors; the people are so warm and happy. Your world is something we never knew existed. We were quite sheltered in the Adephaga..." she paused for a moment as if to digest the magnitude of this observation. "It would be an honour to make this our new home."

"The honour is ours - ahh!" yelped Athiok as Athara touched a sore spot.

"Sorry, Baba."

"So... what of the one chasing your daughter for the stone?"

Elytra looked at him and sighed with relief. "He is no longer a threat." They were silent for a few seconds, but Elytra looked at Athiok nervously, as if she were grappling with what she was about to say next.

"I must ask... for how long...how long before we fight... for what we have left?"

Athiok gazed up at the hut opening, looking at the waxing gibbous moon. "We have until full moon. Days. We need every leader to fight together. The stone alone is not enough, but we do have Loshi."

"What about Loshi?" Elytra responded quizzically.

"She is special, yes? She is the prophecy. It is she who leads us to victory."

Elytra shook her head fervently. "She is only a child, she -"

Athiok raised his hand as if to silence her protestations. "She is brave. True leader. Jakiko chose her to be bearer. We fight WITH her, FOR her. This is the will of the Gods."

Athara placed her hand on top of both of theirs. "Together. We will fight together."

Athiok yawned anticlimactically, and Elytra rose to her feet. "I will leave you to rest now. I will start the training for the archers tomorrow. They will be ready to shoot when the time comes."

"I will send out the message to all. We will meet at sunrise," added Athara.

"Very well."

Elytra exited the hut as Athara covered Athiok with a blanket.

"Rest now, Baba. You need to get your strength back."

As she started to leave, he grabbed her wrist.

"The stones have not been unified for many many moons. We know not of its power..."

Athara nodded and patted his hand assuredly. "Have faith, Baba." She leaned over and kissed his forehead.

"Rest now, I will check on you soon."

* * *

Athara stepped out of the hut and a tri-beetle walked up to her.

"Good morning Athara," the tribeetle respectfully nodded her head. "The Daerra have arrived. They wait for you at the hilltop."

"Very good, I will see them now."

She made her way through a sloping hillside field that rose above the village, leading her to a stone pathway that was lined with flowers. At the end of the path, Athara could see the four butterflies hovering and flapping their delicate wings in loose formation, glorious in their spectacular colors. She couldn't help but smile at their effortless beauty as she approached them, despite the serious nature of the meeting.

"Thank you all for arriving so quickly. As you know, war will soon be upon us and we need to have all leaders to meet at sunrise. In order for this to happen, we need your help in contacting the leaders of the forest."

The butterflies murmured quietly in reaction to this. Athara stepped to a black butterfly with blue and metallic spots on his wings, his body streaked in haphazard crimson stripes. "Rio, you are to contact Arthro, the ruler of the spider legions. We need them all." She retrieved a tiny periwinkle from her hair and pinned it to the base of his left wing. He bowed his head slightly.

"As you wish, it will be done."

Next was a slightly smaller butterfly, its wings a sandy golden color with grey and sepia tones. "Hedy, you are to give the message to Hymon, the Queen of wasps. They are fierce and deadly, and they love a good battle." She pulled a tiny yellow yarrow from her hair and pinned it, as the butterfly nodded in acceptance.

The third butterfly was impressive in size, a silvery blue beauty, and the sunlight shining off its wings made it look like metal. "Lyca, you are to give word to Imago, King of the Cicadas. They are the most dangerous airborne fleet, and we need them with us." She pulled a white galanthus from her hair and pinned it.

"It will be done."

She stepped to the last butterfly. Its wings were a crisp white with brown spots, like dusted cocoa. "Pieri, I give you the greatest challenge of all. This message is to be given to Stajo, leader of the red ant army. The ants will need to be persuaded. Their history with us is a bit...complex."

The butterfly nodded in acceptance. "He will receive your message, I promise you." She pinned a pink lathyrus on the butterfly and stepped back.

"You have all been given a special task that will help determine the fate of this forest. May the Gods protect you in your travels."

The butterflies fluttered off in different directions. Athara watched them intently until they were out of sight, and turned back down the path towards the village.

* * *

Back on the other end of the village, the hammering of stone echoed through the lush green fields as the tribeetles worked diligently on making as many weapons and shields as possible. They pounded and crushed up rocks, grinding them into dust and then mixing with honey and tree saps. They carefully dipped the green stone in each batch to give it strength and then poured the special contents into the spear and arrow head moulds. Others chopped long flower stems and collected them to be placed on hooks and then brushed with this strong lacquer making them unbreakable for sword handles, spears and arrows. Leaves were carved and hardened, thus creating impenetrable shields to withstand even the strongest force.

Metwa was milling about, overseeing the labour. He stopped to talk to a beetle who had finished crafting a sword, and was just about to test its weight when Soura approached him, looking concerned.

"Metwa, have you seen Teok?"

"Not this morning, but I know some of the tribe went east to gather food. May I assist you with something?"

Soura shook her head absently, and surveyed the many beetles slowly as they worked, searching for Teok's face. Her eyes fell upon Aniya who was teaching martial arts to the surviving Adephegans, and she noticed that Loshi wasn't with her. Realizing that both of them were unaccounted for, she turned and quickly walked away through the blades of grass, disappearing into the forest.

* * *

In the orchards south of where the workers were readying the village, Loshi and Teok walked together, gathering fallen berries and collecting their findings in woven baskets. Teok stopped suddenly in his tracks, and looked at Loshi with a curious smile. "Have you ever eaten a rasprie?"

She squinched up her face. "No, what is that?"

"Come follow me, I will show you."

They followed a small path to a row of shrubs with bright red raspberries dangling, the branches bending from the weight of their abundance. He picked up a fallen berry from the ground and cleaned it off, gesturing for her to open her mouth. She recoiled in mock fright, but was still seemingly skeptical about the tiny drupelets.

"Just trust me, it's delicious."

Loshi opened her mouth and he popped the berry in playfully, and stood back to wait for her response. Her eyes widened and she smiled. "It IS delicious!"

Teok chuckled at her reaction. "Did I not tell you? Now, would you like to climb and see who can gather the most berries?"

She squinted and arched her brow. "Are you challenging me, sir? You know I'm the chosen one!"

He rolled his eyes. "Talk is cheap, my lady!" He gestured to two spots on the ground. "This is your pile and this is mine."

Loshi swept her hair back and Teok handed her a dagger.

"Are you ready, oh chosen one?"

"I was born ready!"

He put the blade between his teeth and prepared to climb. She followed suit, and they began their climb up the shrub, slicing and dropping the raspberries to the ground. It wasn't long before Teok noticed she was moving more swiftly than him. Her pile was beginning to peak like a triangle quickly. Not to be easily outdone, he grabbed a raspberry and threw it at Loshi, and it spattered on her shoulder.

She looked at him in mock shock, then grinned and threw one right back in his face and laughed when it burst all over his cheek. They launched into a raspberry war, pelting each other and laughing, dodging each red drupelet as it smattered each other's clothing and faces. Suddenly, Loshi lost her grip and fell to the ground with a splashy thud.

"Loshi!"

He dropped to the ground beside her and shook her shoulders gently. "Loshi!"

Her eyes were closed, she didn't move an inch. Her body lay limp and unresponsive as he continued to try and rouse her.

Just as his concern was turning to panic, Loshi opened her left eye and smiled. He breathes a sigh of relief and they both burst into a fit of laughter, before pausing in a moment of quiet connection. Her eyes locked with his. He moved in close and they kissed gently as Loshi still lay on the ground.

In the distance, Soura watched Teok and Loshi in their tender moment. A tear ran down her cheek, and although it hurt her to watch, she could not look away.

* * *

The Mantuu army ships approached the mountain, moving through the waves towards its imposing base. The sound of water crashing drowned out the painful groans of exhaustion from the rowing Mantuu warriors.

On her ship, Kaiza rested on the tomb of her slain lover as she was suddenly awakened by Kaba. She opened her eyes and looked out at the mountain ahead.

"How much longer?"

Kaba hesitated somewhat nervously before answering. "One more day my Queen. The moon will be full. The boats with catapults are too far away and we need them to catch up, it would be wise to wait for them before we get any closer."

She side-eyed him, displeased yet understanding.

"Very well."

Kaba walked to the front of the boat and raised his hand out to signal the closer boats to halt. Some Mantuu soldiers collapsed in exhaustion, moaning in agony as their weary limbs finally gained reprieve. Kaiza pressed her finger to her lips, and her obedient army was immediately silent.

All was silent, even Kaiza. She cocked her head thoughtfully, as if to listen to some sort of imaginary tune in the distance. She closed her eyes in concentration, and slowly, a grin spread across her face. Kaba stepped to her side, somewhat nervously.

"What is it? What do you see?"

Her eyes opened. A small smile spread across her face.

"Heartbreak."

She lifted her hands to the sky. Her lips parted and her eyes turned red as a little red moth darted out of her mouth and flew toward the mountain.

Part 15

Until Victory or Death

The morning sun began to climb in the sky and the sound of drums echoed through the forest, signaling for all to gather in the village square. In the centre of a soil mound was a nutshell fountain filled with water that sparkled in the sunlight.

Athara stepped to the fountain and looked out at all the beetles and other insects sitting together, awaiting her introduction. Never would she have ever imagined a sight like this. She grinned broadly at the unique and beautiful mix of species that gathered in the audience. For a moment she was almost overwhelmed with emotion, feeling inspired by the idea that insects of all backgrounds, from all parts of the forest, had heeded the call to stand beside their brothers and sisters, many of whom they had never met.

Her smile quickly faded when she was reminded of the circumstances which had brought them together, and the possibility of this union of kinship being short-lived. Here they all waited anxiously in the wake of war, undoubtedly seeking words of encouragement and hope, though they did not speak of it.

Loshi stood by Athara's side and she looked to her mother in the crowd, who smiled with pride. She stepped forward and faced the audience, took a deep breath and exhaled slowly before speaking.

"We are all here to witness the coming of a new age, and to unite in a shared purpose. The coming together of armies that were once adversaries, but are now allies. We come together to fight against an evil unlike anything we have faced before. Our homes, our lives and our futures are in grave danger."

Loshi paused for a moment, pretending not to notice the fear and nervousness on the crowd's faces.

Athara steps in with hope in her voice. 'The prophecy was grim until the Gods intervened and brought us hope. The Seers are no more, they have fallen to an evil entity, and the prophecy is not what they had spoken of. We do not need soothsayers and oracles. We have the courage and the power of unity to take on the wretched forces that come for us. We will fight and die for our lives, for our freedom, for the lives of our children and children's children, if that is what it takes!"

The beetles stomped and roared in rapturous support as Loshi pulled out her sword and raised it up to the sky.

"We will work, prepare and sweat to prevent unnecessary bloodshed on the battlefield. We will inflict terror in them with our courage, our fearlessness. Their greatest error will be their doubt in us, their doubt in our spirit! Chio biraba tiku!"

The crowd erupted in applause again at Loshi's words, which had struck an inspired chord with them all. The applause was hushed when Teok and Metwa emerged, helping a limping Athiok to the fountain. The insects watched with quiet reverence for his will and strength. He took each agonizing step with extreme caution, appearing unsteady, and suddenly fell to one knee, eliciting a collective gasp from the crowd. Teok tried to help him up but Athiok waved him away as he slowly rose back up to his feet, shaking and trembling while straightening his legs.

Suddenly, he threw his cane away and somersaulted and cartwheeled the rest of the way to the fountain. The crowd laughed and cheered at his clever performance, relieved that he had clearly made a full recovery. He bowed to the insects and pulled out the stone that had healed his broken body so quickly.

"The power of the stone is real, yes? My body was broken, but not my soul, not my heart. I lived in this forest my entire life, like you! It is my family, my neighbor, my strength, my dream. My love for our home," he pounded on his heart with his fist. "Unbreakable! Like me!"

Athiok giggled cheekily and bent over to put the stone in the water before taking a few steps back. The water ignited with radiant light in the eyes of every beetle and insect, who stood paralyzed in wonder at what was happening before them. A rhythmic humming sound began to vibrate higher and closer causing everyone to look around in curiosity.

Tiny frogs began to appear and hop out of the blades of grass and the beautiful Blue Frog Queen emerged on her beautiful throne, tied onto the shell of a large turtle slowly pounding the ground. Tiny frogs escorted another turtle which was carrying the second green stone behind her. Everyone watched in awe as she rose up off her throne in levitation and her dark eyes turned to an icy blue glimmer. She lifted her hand toward the stone and it rose up slowly and floated right into Athiok's hand. She smiled at Elytra and gave her a wink.

"To the tribe of Asunta and the beetles of the Adephaga, I am Queen Nurra. I am the leader of Amphibia and Reptilia. I, along with my many and mighty armies, will join in this fight to save our forest."

She floated down and stepped to the rim of the fountain, nodding to Athiok. He placed the second stone in the water and the two stones merged, causing the water to glow with even more brilliance.

She looked at Loshi with strength in her gaze. "We fight with you and for you, stone bearer."

Loshi bowed her head in a gesture of respect. "The honor is mine, great Queen."

All of the sudden, a gigantic striped spider emerged from the greenery, tromping through the grass and startling all the beetles as they all hastily cleared a path for it down the centre of the soil mound. His charcoal colored body and fiery orange haired mandibles made him appear both fierce and valiant. He crawled slowly through the crowd, looking at the beetles with his many black eyes as they gazed back upon him in fear. His body was enormous and heaved with every breath and step he took towards the fountain; he did not say a word, his face was void of expression.

The spider approached the fountain and placed a tiny periwinkle into the water. He looked at Athara and bowed.

"I am Arthro, the King of all Arachna. I received your message and spoke with my advisories on the matter we face. A conclusion was made with great cognizance as time moves closer to conflict. We have a delicate history, our species and yours. But as marked as it is, we also share this forest. Knowing this, we accept this alliance and to put an end to our past contentions."

Loshi beamed with happiness. "We readily accept this alliance."

Before the crowd could respond, a massive wasp and cicada whooshed over the village, buzzing and circling over the fountain. They swooped down, dropping their yellow and white flowers into the fountain. The cicada landed in front of Loshi and its giant wings slowed. It hunched over and gazed at her deeply.

"We live amongst the trees, young beetle, and we have been watching you. The Jakiko has a power like no other and it was you whom they chose. You will risk your life for this forest, child?"

Loshi glanced at her mother and Aniya, and looked back at the Cicadian King. "I would indeed fight and die for this forest, my good King."

He smiled and glanced at the wasp Queen, who nodded her approval. "I believe you will, brave little beetle. I believe you will. You will have my fleet, as well as every clade of the Monophys. We will fight with and for you."

It was at this moment that a panicked murmur had begun to spread through the crowd. Beetles began to pull out their weapons and others scurried for shelter. Teok scanned the crowd for the cause of the commotion. He didn't have to search for long as dozens of red ants descended into the crowd, followed by a leader who appeared both militant and yet cavalier in his demeanor.

Elytra and Aniya stood together with their hands on their weapons. Teok stood beside Loshi protectively as the ants drew closer.

"Who is that?" Loshi whispered under her breath. Teok gripped his sword tightly. "He is Stajo, leader of the Red Ant Army. The most vicious army in the forest, and an enemy to all that live within it."

Stajo advanced towards Athiok and stood tall with his hands behind his back, peering down his nose at him. "It has come to my attention that you wish to unify our forces amidst this impending conflict.

Tell me, why would my soldiers risk their lives to fight alongside our enemies?"

Stajo paused for an answer, but Athiok was silent, unflinching and calm.

"The Mantuu are a robust army and we cannot withstand their numbers. Even if we all fight together, we are still outnumbered. Why would you put the lives of your species in the hands of -"

"Because of her!" Teok interjected, gesturing to Loshi.

Stajo's eyes widened slightly and he stepped closer to Loshi as if to inspect her.

"This little beetle? You risk the fate of all insects for her? She is a child!"

"She has been chosen by the Jakiko to lead us to battle," said Athiok.

Stajo gave a slight scoff under his breath, and shook his head as he slowly circled Loshi, continuing to size her up. "Your mythological nonsense has plagued your beetles for centuries." He stopped circling and stood directly beside Loshi. She continued staring right ahead while Stajo drew closer to her, so close that she could practically feel his breath on her cheek.

"What is so special about you?" he asked, flicking a small leaf off of her hair. Without a word, she grabbed his hand pulling it toward her and downward, twisting his body towards the ground and hyper-rotating his limb into a modified arm lock. The red ants immediately moved to strike and the beetles stepped to them in defiance without missing a beat. Loshi pushed his arm back, and he glowered at her menacingly.

"I am the daughter of the late King Tearon, son and heir to the throne of King Dynastis. I am the princess of a mighty fallen Kingdom, and a pupil of the last great combat master General Hillius. I did not seek this fate for myself! I have lost my father, my teacher, my youth, and my home to a battle for these stones, but I will not lose my forest. I will not have these and the sacrifices of so many others be in vain. Now, are you with us, or against us?"

Stajo looked to the red ants and nodded at them, as if to signal them to back away. As they stepped back, he effortlessly broke out of her grip, knocking her to the ground and smiled wryly.

"Forgive me, little beetle. I needed to be sure of your bravery and commitment to this cause."

He chuckled to himself, pulled the pink lathyrus flower from his collar and placed it in the water.

"Your role in this battle is an extraordinary one, little beetle. It would be an honor to fight alongside you."

Loshi glanced at her mother who, unbeknownst to her, had her bow and arrow raised the entire time, aimed straight at Stajo. Seeing her daughter's reassuring look, Elytra eased the tension on her bow and dropped it to her side.

Athiok beamed with pride at the significant alliance that had just been formed, hopefully putting to rest many years of delicate relations. "Now, Loshi... place stone in water. Now, three become one, in power and beauty."

Loshi stepped to the glowing fountain and pulled off her ring while everyone watched in anticipation. She dropped it into the water, which began to ripple and bubble, rolling as if it was a pot on boil. Slowly but steadily, the stones came together in the centre of the fountain bowl in a brilliant light, gleaming like a fallen star.

Athiok looked over the edge of the fountain bowl, and the water slowly calmed. He cupped his hand over the fountain, dipping it into the glowing water and raising it to his face.

"With this water, I make an oath to you all. Commitment to brotherhood, to fight as one. Together, until death or victory!"

He drank and stepped back as Stajo stepped forward and dipped his hand in.

"Until death or victory!"

Queen Nurra stepped forward, and the spider King Arthro. Then Queen Hymon and King Imago. All cupped their hands into the water and drank from it in a symbolic gesture of their commitment to the shared oath.

Then it was Loshi's turn. She stepped to the fountain and scooped the last remaining drops from the bowl, raising it up and letting it roll off her hand and into her mouth. She smiled at Athiok and the rest of the leaders. "It is d-"

Loshi was interrupted by a falling ash upon her nose. "You have got to be kidding me."

Flying above was the black and white striped butterfly, who raised his bushy eyebrows at the sight below.

"Well, would ya look at this! There's a party, and we wasn't invited!" Behind him dozens of the butterflies appeared, looking exaggeratedly dapper in their slicked back hair and caterpillar-like mustaches.

"You cats might wanna refill that fountain, cuz you ain't done yet. This is just as much our home as it is yours, see?"

At that, earwigs, centipedes and aphids appeared in clusters, and Athiok joyously filled the fountain for all to partake.

With this moment, history was made. Leaders of all insect species, some longtime brethren and some newfound allies, drank and committed to unity. After that, not a moment was wasted as they strategized and finalized their plans for the impending battle. They conferred long into the night about how each army's strengths could be utilized, and any potential challenges they would face. Training would begin at sunrise and although the soldiers should have been fast asleep in preparation, very few would be able to shut their eyes.

Despite the palpable anxiety in the village, the night was peaceful and quiet. Loshi slept alone in a leafy hut, guarded by two heavily armed beetles. The green stone laid beside her as she closed her eyes in an attempt to nod off. Suddenly, the stone began to vibrate and pulsate, flashing intermittently in an ominous glow. The flickering woke her instantly and she sat up with a jolt.

Outside Loshi's hut, one guard noticed a flickering in the darkness and nudged the other. "Look there - do you see that?"

The other guard narrowed his eyes, trying to see into the vast darkness that blanketed the village.

"I see nothing."

"Look closer...we are being watched."

The guard placed his hand on his sword as he took a cautious step towards the darkness. The other guard covered him from behind. Far ahead in the distance, so small that an untrained eye would have missed it, were a pair of tiny red eyes. They could have easily passed for a pair of flickering fireflies hovering in the distance.

"Who goes there? Show yourself at once!"

At that, the eyes disappeared and inside the hut, the green stone stopped oscillating. A moment later, Loshi stepped out from the opening cautiously. "Is everything alright? Is something out there?"

The guards still were looking into the darkness, trying to mask their confusion.

"If there was, it's gone now, Princess." She studied their faces for a moment, and followed their gaze. Seeing only blackness, Loshi finally went inside. She laid back down, clutching the stone close to her heart, staring at the wall for some time before closing her eyes again.

Part 16

Love, on the Brink of War

The early morning fog had settled. A brisk wind picked up as the sun began to rise over the easterly hills of the village. Hundreds of beetles were already hard at work, training for combat. The bees, wasps and cicadas practiced continuous flight drills with archers on their backs as they fired at targets etched into the ground. Elytra sat on the back of the Wasp Queen Hymon hovering overhead, commanding when and where to target and shoot. After dozens upon dozens of rounds, they were satisfied with their soldiers' performance.

Elytra tapped Hymon moment midair and called up to her, "I may have an idea that could help optimize our attack. Come, we'll head east." The Wasp Queen turned to her soldiers and instructed them to continue with the drills. At that, the two Queens flew away into the sun as the insects carried on.

On the field, Metwa, Teok and many other tribeetles trained the ground forces with dagger and sword practices. Hand to hand combat and kill shot drills were relentlessly taught and executed to perfection. They walked among the soldiers, eyeing their technique and correcting for effectiveness where necessary.

Without warning, Teok came to an abrupt stop in front of one of the soldiers who was familiar to him, even under armor. He looked closer at her eyes and suddenly, the beetle turned her head sharply and glared at him bitterly.

"Soura?" He stepped back and his face softened, as if somehow wordlessly acknowledging that there was a difference in her.

"Where have you been? When did you learn how to fight?"

She smirked at him dryly. "I have been here, you have been preoccupied. Perhaps, busy picking raspries?"

If Teok felt any guilt, he did not show it; instead he stepped back towards her and gently stretched out his hand in a conciliatory manner. She struck it away angrily, which caught the attention of the other soldiers.

"I don't want to fight with you, Soura - this is ridiculous."

"Why? Are you afraid you'll look weak in front of your girlfriend?" Soura swung at him and Teok deftly dodged the blow before returning the strike. She blocked it, jabbed his side and kicked him to the ground. She brought her leg down hard in an axe kick as he rolled out of the way, and she dropped to her knee. He barely had enough time to straighten up and catch his breath before she catapulted herself toward him and speared him to the ground, striking him hard in the mouth.

"A bit hard to kiss with a busted lip, I imagine!"

She attempted to punch him again but he grabbed the back of her hair and flipped her backwards to the ground. She landed hard on her stomach with a thud creating a cloud of dust. He climbed to his feet as she stumbled and rose up to face him. Soura's anger had only intensified. It was palpable, and the crowd of soldiers that had gathered were excited at what they had witnessed.

She stepped closer to Teok but he raised his hand to halt her. "Enough," he croaked out, and he turned his head away. In an instant she was in front of him, and he felt the cold hard blade of her sword pressed into his abdomen, directly over his heart. He grabbed her hand with his, pushing the blade slightly into himself and watching as her anger began to turn to tears.

"Well? Are you going to kill me, Soura?"

She jerked back her sword and stalked off through the crowd before anyone could see her tears begin to roll down her cheeks. She sighed shakily, and then sharply, whispering to herself under her breath.

"You will regret this."

* * *

The training ground was loud and energetic as Loshi arrived at Aniya's hut to meet for training. Seeing no sign of her, she tapped on the door.

"Aniya, are you awake?"

Silence. Then, a small commotion coming from inside the hut.

"Aniya!!"

"YES! Um...I mean, just a minute!" yelped Aniya, somewhat muffled. Loshi sighed in exasperation, and peeked through the small opening in the door. At that second, Aniya popped her head up. "I will be out in just a moment, I promise."

A few moments later, Aniya joined Loshi at the foot of the path, adjusting her armor and fastening her belt with her daggers holstered. She glanced back quickly at the hut and apologized again to Loshi, who pretended not to notice Metwa as he slipped out the door of the hut quietly. Loshi smirked and nudged Aniya playfully.

"What? What are you smiling at?"

"You, silly. You're in love!"

Aniya feigned surprise but could barely keep a straight face before bursting into a fit of giggles. "I am in love!" She fell backward dramatically and landed on the leaf of a shrub. Loshi lay back beside her, and they gazed at the clouds rolling by. Aniya looked at Loshi quizzically. "And, what about you, Princess?"

Loshi stifled a big grin. "Well...we kissed."

"Ha! I knew it!" exclaimed Aniya as she shot up. Her face beamed, but her smile quickly faded. "I can't believe we are in love, and we both could potentially die tomorrow."

"Ugh. I know...isn't it romantic?" They both slumped back down into the leaf and stared off into the clouds.

"Ahem! Shouldn't you two be training?" The stern voice startled them and they jumped to their feet to see the tiny blue Frog Queen standing in front of them.

"Forgive us your highness. We were just taking a break," stammered Loshi.

The Frog Queen was unimpressed. "Follow me," she said.

They followed the tiny blue Frog Queen as she led them to a hilltop where Athiok stood, looking stern. She hopped forward and pressed her fingers to her temples as her eyes glow a vivid crystal blue. Each serpent, frog, and turtle's eyes began to glow as she began to see through each of their eyes, searching everywhere through the forest, though not saying a word about what for.

Within moments, the Frog Queen's eyes widened slightly in a look of silent shock. From the eyes of an unassuming tree frog that was resting high above the treetops, she had caught a glimpse of the Mantuu ships approaching in the distance. She took her fingers slowly from her temples, blinked the blue from her eyes, and looked at Athiok gravely.

"They will reach land by sunrise; we must be ready."

Athiok let out a small exhale and looked at Loshi with a small smile.

"This your time, Loshi. The fate of all is in your hands. Time to lead your legions as you are meant to." Athiok held out his hands to Aniya and Loshi. "Now, help an old beetle down the hill and get to work!"

The two girls nodded and escorted the elder beetle down the hill as Queen Nurra pressed on her temples again. Unbeknownst to the group, a small slithering snake had emerged from a shrub and slithered slowly around a tree, moving its way up the trunk. Its eyes then turned blue and suddenly it saw two red eyes in the darkness, deep inside a knotted hole in the tree. The eyes were watching them. The Frog Queen snapped out of her trance and was visibly startled as she realized that they were, in fact, not alone.

* * *

Queen Elytra and Queen Hymon soared over the Adephagen landscape, seeing the devastation by the flooding and genocidal battle that had taken place. A once beautiful landscape, now marred by destruction.

"What happened here?" Queen Hymon exclaimed.

Queen Elytra, with tears in her eyes, said nothing in response. Hymon nodded slowly, understanding Elytra's unspoken grief that can only come from loss.

Elytra spotted the palace, and gestured to Hymon. "Down there, to your left."

Hymon swooped down and landed on the ground beside the crumbled remains of what used to be a castle wall. The ground was still saturated from the rain and mud mixed with the blood of beetles both deceased and injured. Decaying bodies littered the castle grounds; weapons and armor were strewn about like acorns. It was as if an explosion went off, obliterating everything and everyone in its wake.

Hymon surveyed the destruction in awe, then shook her head in dismay. "This was once a mighty empire. Now, it's a gravesite.

A cornerstone of this forest, now a relic of history because of that stone."

Elytra walked over to one of the broken rafts and picked up one of the poisonous glass balls.

"This is why we have come here."

Hymon approached cautiously. "What is it?"

"This is the deadliest weapon I have witnessed in battle."

"What does it do?"

Elytra walked over to a large decaying Mosquito and placed the ball on its chest.

"Step back," she cautioned.

Hymon stepped back and watched Elytra intently. Elytra pulled an arrow from her pouch and raised it up. She aimed and fired swiftly, smashing the ball in two and pouring the liquid all over the dead insect. As the liquid spread like molten lava, the insect disintegrated. There was nothing left but ash after several seconds and Hymon was horrified.

"How is this possible? Who created these?"

Elytra said nothing at first and approached the pile of ash, examining it. "In the wrong hands, the stone can create evil beyond imagination."

Wordlessly, they packed the rest of the poison glass balls in a wasp sack, and headed back to share what they had found.

* * *

The sun was setting on the village and the leaders had gathered together outside Athiok's hut to go over final plans for battle. They all sat circled around a thin branch and leaf table with the top layered with dirt to be drawn on. There were cut pieces of leaves painted in different colors to be placed on the map, representing the various armies and tribes.

Athiok stood up and the leaders' conversation lowered to a murmur.

"Thank you for being here. The eve of war is upon us. We have much to do. Who would like to begin?"

Arthro took a thin stem and drew the mountain first, then the trees representing the Black Forest.

"This is where we should draw them in to fight, in this forest where the fallen Kings lay. We will web out bridges from tree to tree for constant movement for the archers. They must shoot and move. They must always be moving."

He paused as he moved around the table and drew a series of dashes.

"The Mantuu will attack the trees, that is for certain. We will also do our best to barricade the bottom of the mountain to try and slow them down."

Stajo then leaned in, drawing lines toward the mountain.

"That gives us the opportunity to storm the mountain - overwhelm them. I have three thousand ants ready to attack. If we can rush the first wave of their ground forces from the front, that's when the air attacks can take care of their archers in the middle."

Imago stepped forward, pinning stems on the mountains.

"We can carry two beetles at a time, dropping them off on the mountain and from there we can take out their infantry from behind, killing them from both ends."

Just then, Elytra and Hymon landed a few feet away. The leaders turned to look at them as they approached the table, somewhat out of breath. Elytra approached the dirt plan that was being drawn out and placed one of the poisonous glass balls on the table. They all looked in wondrous confusion.

"This will end the war. If we can drop these and kill the sorceress, it will break the curse her army is under. If she dies, the war is over."

The Blue Frog Queen stepped in, putting her hand on the ball. Then quickly backs away feeling its danger. Elytra takes the ball placing it down safe from them all. The frog Queen adds tiny dots above the trees.

"That is presuming she has no defense against our air fleet. It will be dangerous for the wasps and bees, but it is crucial that we try."

Athiok drew a line from the centre down. "If the ants can make an opening through the centre, then Loshi and the rest of us can ride on through splitting in all directions."

Elytra looked over at the butterfly as he blew smoke across the table. He fluttered down and drew a number of lines far from the battle ground, closer to the village.

"You bugs are acting like you won this war already, but anything can change! We need a crew to keep the dame with the stone safe. The evil thing will be coming for her in no time flat." The butterfly's cigar bobbed up and down as he continued. "Me and my boys along with the Earwigs and the Aphids will hold back close to the girl, in case things don't go as planned. Can't be too prepared, see?"

He placed his cigar where the village was drawn on the map. "I'll go let them know we got some loading up to do."

He took off, and the leaders leaned back in their seats. Stajo stood tall, looking pleased with the meeting.

"Very well, I will brief my commanding units and we will be ready for tomorrow. Sleep easy tonight comrades."

He excused himself from the meeting, and one by one, the other leaders followed, knowing fully the weight of the day that lay ahead.

The moonlight shines its beautiful glow on the village as Loshi sits on a small branch of a tree. She admires the insects that have no problem sleeping this night. She holds the ring in her hand and thinks about this moment and everything that led her to now. She hears a ruffle of leaves as Teok appears. She is happy to see him and smiles. "Am I disturbing you Loshi?" She shakes her head "No not at all, come sit." They sit for a while as she puts her head on his shoulder. He feels her nervousness of what tomorrow brings as he hides his well. He nudges her as she smiles. "What is it?" "Remember when I said that I did not have anything to remind me of my mother by? Well, I do have one thing" He opens his hand and reveals a beautiful intertwined bracelet made to shimmer like gold. "I have been saving this my whole life to give to whom I love. Who I would die for and live for." He puts it on her wrist and she puts her hand on his face. They move in slow and kiss in-front of the brilliant glow of the moon.

Part 17

A Crack in the Heavens

Dawn had not yet broken when Kaiza and her Mantuu ships reached the shore. The boats carrying the catapults kept their proper range in distance, hundreds of them battered and broken from days spent battling the relentless waves. Kaba stepped to her side timidly.

"The soldiers will need a moment of rest. They are visibly exhausted. Give them time and they will honor you with bloodshed."

Kaiza looked out at her fleet solemnly. "Let them rest, there will be a change in plans."

"Are we not to storm the mountain?"

She turned and looked at Kaba with determination. "They are waiting for us to do exactly that. Load up the catapults."

"As you wish."

He left to brief the army her as she stared at the mountain with an ominous grin. She tapped the tomb lightly with her fingers.

"Soon my love. Very soon."

* * *

Daylight shone over the horizon to reveal spider webs streamed across the trees, glistening like shiny crystal ribbons. The web-woven wall at the base of the mountain was so tall and strong that not even the mightiest wind could make it budge. As armies began to migrate and meet at the base, the ground began to tremble slightly and thousands of red ants appeared, approaching the Black Forest and combing through the land. Red ants with razor sharp mandibles ready to rip and tear any opposition to pieces.

Arthro and Stajo met at the base and exchanged pleasantries, and they both looked up at the giant grey mountain. Stajo's eyes darted between the webbing in the trees and the grand webbed wall, nodding with satisfaction.

"An impressive structure."

Arthro glanced at his spider troops, satisfied at this response, and then back to Stajo.

"You didn't expect anything less, did you, comrade?"

Stajo smirked dryly at this.

Back in the village, the wasps and bees were readying themselves for takeoff. One hundred glass balls were strapped to each of the bees, and an archer perched on every back. Hundreds of them hovered as Hymon rose to their level in the air.

"My warriors, we own these skies. Be precise in your every shot, and with every sting. I see the fear in your eyes, the dread at what waits for us. But death does not come for us today! No - today we are the takers of lives! Today we defend, we kill, for your sons and your daughters, and your forest!"

The winged insects buzzed and cheered loudly and with that, they flew off into the clouds. Elytra, with her face and body striped with red war paint, jumped on Hymon's back and looked at Loshi and Aniya.

"My love for you is stronger than you could ever imagine, my dear, and I trust that you will endure whatever comes your way."

She leaned down and grabbed Loshi's hand.

"Loshi be who you are meant to be, and you will know what to do. You are the power, you are stronger than any stone. And Aniya...you be careful, and don't ever leave her side. No matter what."

Aniya nodded, showing her courage. "I promise, my Queen."

Elytra then looked over at Teok with a stare that said so much without saying a word. He nodded silently, and with that, she took off. Imago and his cicada troops followed behind them with two infantry beetles on each back.

The pounding of turtles walking shook the ground as they moved like tanks toward the centre of the field. The turtles wore helmets made of rose thorns meant to smash and pierce like spiked bulldozers. Queen Nurra emerged from the top of a hill, followed by the toads and snakes that slithered up the sides. She looked at Loshi, her eyes turning their light crystal blue as hundreds of tiny topaz-colored frogs appeared in the trees, making them look like blooming jewels.

Athiok rode in on a dignified looking toad, standing strong with a new staff built from a fallen tree leaf stem. He looked at everyone with uncharacteristic solemnity, his face and torso glowing with white and periwinkle streaks of color.

"The hour is upon us." He scanned the silent army slowly before landing directly at Loshi.

"Are you ready, stone bearer?"

"I am ready" Loshi answered evenly, looking every bit the warrior in her magenta and icy blue war paint.

Teok approached her side, giving her a look of incitement. "Your army is ready Loshi. They are under your command - we fight with and for you."

Loshi took a deep breath and ascended the high hill that looked out over the masses of insects that had assembled under her this day. She looked at the remaining commanders, and became nervous. She froze. Feeling panicked, she looked to Aniya, who mouthed the words "Say something!"

Loshi closed her eyes and thought of her father, and General Hillius. She thought of all they had taught her, and all she had lost in their deaths. She thought about the Adephaga and what was left of her beautiful home. The beautiful home of so many, many of whom were washed away with the kingdom itself. She felt the bracelet given to her from Teok and felt an overwhelming feeling of courage. She opened her eyes and gazed out at the crowd, clutching the stone in her hand.

"On this ground our fathers stood against the Ants and defended our freedom. If we must fight amongst the fallen kings, then we must live up to the sacrifices they made so that we could be here today. We must extinguish the evil that brings danger to our forests. It comes for this stone, and for our homes and our lives. It has brought us together for the first time, our many different species of insects, all fighting a common enemy for our right to live. To thrive without terror, or fear! The Jakiko has been in my bloodline for centuries, as well as yours, and it has chosen me to lead us into the darkness. Together, we will block out the darkness with the light of our bravery! Together, we end this tyranny once and for all!"

The soldiers roared and stomped their feet, banging on their armor in spirited unity. The commanders slammed their weapons against their chests and against the ground in a rare display of trepidation. Aniya beamed with pride and admiration, as did Teok. With a final cry and her fist raised high in the air, the army began their march.

* * *

Kaiza stood on the beach facing the mountain with hundreds of boats behind her, casting a fearsome visage on anyone who dared to face her. The Mantuu army awaited her command; their bodies and souls had been held captive and tortured under her relentless pursuit of the stone.

Kaba returned to her side after meeting with the enslaved Mantuu, looking visibly irate and bothered. His eyes were not red, which meant he was not a captive under her sorcery. The weight of the consequences of his jealousy was heavy upon him. He swallowed his anger.

"The catapults are filled and ready to fire. We await your orders."

Kaiza smiled slightly. She opened her palms outwards at her side and raised them slowly. She began to radiate a deep scarlet glow which made the Mantuu's eyes glow even brighter in unison. Their limbs began to grow longer and broader, which made them scream in pain.

"Behind that mountain is your freedom! Retrieve the stone and I will release you. You will not have fought in vain, you will kill for your salvation, power, and freedom. It is yours for the taking!"

They growled and barked like starved wolves, their saliva pooling from their mouths on the boat deck. She looked at Kaba who was standing near the bow, and walked over to share his view..

"The insect armies await us to storm down that mountain; are the catapults ready?"

"Yes, at your command," Kaba replied, expressionless.

Kaiza raised her arms in front of her, aiming at what awaited. "Let's give them a deadly surprise. Tear that mountain down."

Kaba turned and signaled. "Fire!"

One by one, dozens of catapults ignited, launching thousands of boulders and sharp rocks through the air towards the mountain, so dense that daylight grew dimmer as they hurtled in front of the sun.

On the other side of the mountain, the ants and spiders awaited their enemy, staring up in anticipation at the colossal mound and scanning for the first sight of Mantuu. The beetles and frogs in the trees listened and watched. Nothing.

Suddenly, a frog soldier alerted the comrades around him. "Listen!"

They listened closely and within seconds, they heard it - a whistling in the distance that grew louder and louder.

Suddenly, an earth-shattering blast startled everyone. They craned their necks frantically to locate the impact but could see nothing.

Elytra yelled up at the archers in the trees. "Eyes open, arrows ready!" The bees and wasps flew higher but saw nothing. Imago and his troops landed on the tops of the trees ready to attack.

The second two dozen Mantuu catapults fired again, whistling through the air, this time smashing into the peak of the mountain and breaking the top off into pieces. The mountain began to rumble and shake as huge boulders rolled down the slopes.

Arthro yelled back at his army, "Get ready! Here they come!"

Stajo looked up the range and saw the rocks rolling down towards the army below. "It's not the Mantuu! Take cover!"

Massive boulders smashed through the webbed barricade and rolled into crowds of running ants and spiders. Another thunderous explosion went off, this time feeling like an earthquake as sunlight came through the cracks in the mountain. Enormous rocks hurtled through the air like meteors and crashed on impact, slowly demolishing the centre of the mountain and sending rubble down the side. Trees were split through their trunks and toppled over, throwing dozens of archers to the ground. The cicadas sprang into action and flew up the side of the trees to retrieve as many archers as they could and bring them to safety.

Another smash leveled the mountain and the sun shone completely through, revealing the devastation. Light hit the Black Forest for the first time in centuries. Stajo frantically scanned through the damage looking for any with signs of life, before coming upon Arthro who was half crushed by a boulder. Blood trickled from his mouth as he tried to speak, but was unable to. Stajo knelt down and held his hand.

"We lived as enemies, but we will die as comrades. The Gods await you, brave leader."

Arthro squeezed his hand as he breathed his final breath. Stajo paused to digest what had just happened, so quickly and yet so calamitous. He straightened up to see that the surviving ants and spiders had begun to regroup. He appeared visibly bothered, and then angry; he pivoted on his heel to face who remained.

"Archers, back to your stations! Infantry, prepare to fight. Time for dinner, boys...on the menu, Mantuu!"

* * *

Back at the village, the aphids stood guard as Athara sat with the women and children who stayed behind in close quarters. The butterflies kept watch from above, fully prepared and ready to protect.

A knock at Athara's hut door startled her, and she slowly opened the door.

"Oh Cofia, you startled me! Please come in."

A pretty tribeetle with a worrisome look on her face entered the hut, and hugged Athara.

"I'm sorry to disturb you, but it's Soura. She has not been herself as of late, and I have not seen her in days…"

"What do you mean? Is she in danger?"

Cofia shook her head. "I don't know. She has been acting odd and very distant. She won't talk to me about it."

Hearing this, Athara sat her down. "I think I know what is wrong, and I believe it has something to do with Teok."

"No no, it's not that. Here - I was cleaning her room and I found this." She reached into her garment pocket and laid a dead red moth on the table.

Athara's calm turned to worry. "A red moth. I must warn the others in the army. Please stay here with the children. I must go quickly."

Before Cofia could utter a word, Athara ran out and waved her arms frantically at the butterfly over her hut to get his attention. He swooped down quickly, and she explained what was happening and showed him the dead moth in her hand. His eyes opened wide in silent concern. At that, she jumped onto his back and flew off toward the Black Forest.

Part 18

The Falling of Stars

Though the morning sun was in the sky, one could barely see it through the blanket of dust and debris that had settled like a thick heavy fog. Kaiza appeared through the crevasse and slowly scanned the army below before her glowing red eyes found Loshi. She grinned diabolically. Loshi returned her gaze with a cold glare and raised her sword.

"Javelin and archers - prepare to fire on my command!"

Metwa and his army gripped their spears, ready to launch their assault. The beetles and frogs in the trees pulled their arrows back and awaited the word. Loshi and Stajo glanced at each other, wordlessly knowing what needed to be done.

Kaiza raised her staff and pointed to Loshi as thousands of red eyes appeared from behind her. She dropped her arm, signaling her army to attack. They swarmed the rocky boulders with viciously eager appetites for what stood in front of them, rushing past Kaiza and descending toward Loshi and her army.

Loshi stood firm with steely calm, even as the thousands of Mantuu were closer and closer.

"Hold!"

Yards away, then feet. Within seconds, their massive size and terrifying gnarls were growing more and more imposing, moving closer and closer.

"Hold!"

They were seconds away. Elytra and the hundreds of Bees and Wasps hovered tensely overhead, poised to attack. Elytra pulled back her bow.

"Aim for their eyes, for they are heartless!"

Loshi hollered her command. Thousands of spears and arrows blanketed the sky, pulverizing packs of Mantuu, skewering them three to four at a time. However, it seemed to make little difference as throngs of Mantuu continued to rush the army.

Archers shot with deathly precision and darted swiftly from tree to tree. Stajo roared loudly, his bellow echoing through the forest as the ants and spiders charged ahead. But the Mantuu overpowered the Ants and Spiders, stampeding through them, leaving a bloody mess in their wake. The Ants try to attack but before they could, the Mantuu were upon them, ripping and tearing limbs and mandibles off their bodies.

Within moments, Stajo's officers, who were last in the line of protection of the leader, found themselves facing off against the Mantuu. They swung their weapons viciously, stabbing and swiping them at the bloodthirsty insects whose red eyes were void of any insectanity or emotion. They blocked, struck back, shielded, and did everything they could to protect the inner circle that was becoming smaller and smaller as the last of Stajo's officers were picked off one by one.

All of a sudden, Stajo found himself surrounded by the vicious insects. He shifted back slowly, keeping on his toes, anticipating where the attack would come from. Left, right, left. He moved lightly on his feet, but it was futile.

They attacked all at once, mercilessly ravaging the commander, ripping his arms from his body and stabbing his left eye in the scuffle. Stajo put up a fight but knew he was powerless against so many. Once they had rendered the mighty commander helpless, the Mantuu held him up victoriously as Kaiza descended the mountain towards them. Stajo looked at her and smiled as blood dripped from his mouth.

"You will not win, sorceress. She is more powerful than you will ever be."

Kaiza's pace quickened and she stalked towards him in fury. She raised her staff up and behind her like a spear, and launched it through Stajo's skull between the eyes, killing him instantly.

At that, all hell broke loose. Nurra and her Turtles rushed forward as Athiok and the Toads followed close behind. The Mantuu archers shot back, picking off Wasps and Bees in the sky and sending them crashing to the ground. The Cicadas landed and dropped beetles on the ground who rushed the Mantuu's to fight sword to sword. The Cicadas ascended again, flew a loop in the air, then hurtled back down towards the earth and spiraled through crowds of Mantuu like suicide bombers. Some were caught and killed, others escaped and flew back upwards.

A high pitched whirring sound could be heard overhead as the wasps flew above, then bobbed and weaved over the Mantuu army, grabbing and piercing them as others were taken down and killed by brute force. Nurra stormed through the mayhem with turtles smashing through the enemy, pulverizing them in a bloody mess. They stampeded the Mantuu out of the way, moving closer and closer to Kaiza who stood her ground calmly beside the impaled head of their mighty slain leader.

Athiok fought the red-eyed predators using his staff as a bow, picking them off one after the next. The snakes stayed closed to the ground undetected, slithering between the stomping feet and dust before grabbing several Mantuu at a time and squeezing the life out of them before they could even react.

Kaiza wordlessly raised her staff up high and opened her mouth, releasing hundreds of red moths into the air and scattering out toward the turtles, toads and snakes. Athiok and Nurra looked on in horror as the red moths attacked the powerful reptiles and amphibians in tornado-like swarms, overwhelming them before they collapsed to the ground. The moths only leaving piles of skeleton when finished devouring them.

Seeing this, Hymon looked back at Elytra. "What say you, Queen? Shall we?" Elytra glanced down at the moths and the carnage below before raising her bow in the air and spinning it, signaling a number of Bees to fly overhead.

"Look up!" Athiok cried out to Nurra in exasperation. She looked up quickly, then jumped onto Athiok's back and they took off. Kaiza observed them soaring through the air and chuckled to herself.

"You will perish like the rest!"

Suddenly, she saw something drop from the air onto one of her soldiers, turning them to dust. Then another, and another. She looked up to see the bees flying overhead and dropping the poisonous glass balls on their targets. Kaiza glanced around, seemingly confused, as the balls landed on the red moths who fizzled and fried them to a near ash.

Elytra spun her bow again as the second round of Bees flew overhead. Kaiza signaled the Mantuu archers to fire at the bees, hitting them as the balls landed below. Some of the Bees managed to dodge the arrows and immediately regrouped, hurtling down to the earth and crashing into the Mantuu archers, effectively killing themselves as well.

In the aftermath of these suicide missions, there was nothing left but mounds of dust as Elytra and Hymon gazed out sadly at the sacrifice made by the bees. Kaiza advanced with her Mantuu army as ash fell like snow across the battlefield. Exhausted and depleted, Elytra and the rest fell back.

* * *

The light of the sun, barely visible, had begun to fall in the sky. Kaba slowly traversed the battle grounds, dragging the tomb of his dead brother behind him. As he stopped for a moment's rest, seeing thousands of dead insects piled on the ground, he realized the magnitude of what had occurred. He began to shake and lose his breath in shock, and dropped the tomb before falling to his knees in despair. He dragged his hand through the grass beneath his knees and raised it to his face, seeing that it was soaked in blood. He steadied himself on the coffin leaving a bloody print on its lid.

"What hell have I caused here..." Kaba whispered to himself, before slowly rising to his feet. He grabbed the ropes and continued onward, dragging the tomb through the remnants of the slaughter.

* * *

Athiok and Nurra stood with Loshi as Elytra and Hymon landed. Elytra looked perplexed.

"The sorceress and her army will approach us within moments. Our casualties are many and her army greatly outnumbers us. Loshi, this is your moment. Are you ready?"

Loshi clenched her jaw slightly at this, understanding what it meant, then nodded bravely. At that, Aniya whipped out her daggers. Teok and Metwa stood shoulder to shoulder with her, showing their allegiance. There was only the sound of the wind whipping through the now wasteland, and the faint cries of fallen infantrymen.

Then, Kaiza appeared. Her body vibrated with an eerie red glow. Hundreds of glowing red eyes surrounded her as she approached them slowly, menacingly, a vile smile upon her lips. At that moment, Aniya approached Loshi, grabbed her hand and turned to face her.

"I love you and I honor you. You are my best friend, and I cherish the life I have had with you and your family. I have always known you were special, as did Master Hillius. So, I think it's time to show this wretched shrew who she's messing with."

Loshi squeezed her hand in acknowledgement, holding Aniya's gaze for a few seconds. She then turned her gaze to the sorceress in front of her and stepped forward. Kaiza scoffed lightly, seeing Loshi's confidence but unimpressed by it, and ordered her army to advance. She aimed her staff forward "Zooonda".

The Mantuu ran towards Loshi, who stood with her feet firmly planted. She quickly slipped the ring onto her finger. The three stones united once again, giving Loshi a power like no other. Within seconds, her body was consumed by a green glow, the ring's power vibrating so high, it could be felt by all. Her armor and helmet glistened like white lightning, and her sword was a glowing comet. She took a few slow steps towards her prey, and then took off like a rocket, exploding in a blitzkrieg of violence. Her left hand was like a cannon, releasing blasts of energy that blew Mantuu's apart like a missile blasts. In her right hand, she swung her mighty sword, slicing four to five Mantuu at a time.

Aniya followed suit, working her daggers swiftly and skillfully, one after the other. Teok and Metwa flanked the girls on either end, skewering any Mantuu in their path and showing no mercy. They fought side by side with a laser sharp focus, almost machine-like, slaughtering every enemy soldier without mercy or pause in a physical act of catharsis, having just experienced so much suffering, so much destruction.

One by one, the Mantuu were picked off by the group, their bloody corpses forming small piles in the way of the insect assassins. Suddenly, Kaiza found herself alone and facing Loshi and her army. Athiok stepped forward.

"Sorceress, you have lost. Surrender."

Kaiza fell to her knees and began weeping, to Loshi's surprise. Her shoulders shook with every sob, and she raised her head to look at Loshi. Her weeping then turned to a malicious cackle as she took her staff and spun it upside down, stabbing it into the earth. The ground began to shake and red smoke seeped out of the black soil.

The plants and flowers began to die and crumple, as well as the leaves on the trees before they crinkled and fell. The decayed bodies of the Dead Kings began to slowly rise up from the black earth. Kaiza climbed to her feet and raised her hands to the sky.

"Sarromatha diolakuru sebtoe panu!"

The Dead Kings straightened their bent and broken corpses, shaking dust and soil from their bodies as they began to march forward. Ancient Ants and Beetles, decomposed and withered, stared through Loshi with no life in their eyes. Kaiza stepped forward with confidence.

"Zarathu piku!"

They released their swords and began to stomp toward Loshi, who had paused to regain her focus and realized what she was looking at. Just then, Nurra and Athiok looked up and saw a twinkle in the night sky. Suddenly the stars in the heavens began to trickle down, catching everyone's attention. The tiny balls of light fell further and further, closer and closer.

Loshi looked at Aniya frantically. "What is it?"

Aniya smiled. "It's a friend."

Glowing clumps of neon suddenly shot through the air and landed on the Dead Kings with a "splat!" blinding them as they tried to swat away the oncoming fluorescent chunks hitting their faces.

The sparkling fireflies were carrying acorns, rubbing them on their backsides and throwing them down, smashing the heads of the walking dead.

Queen Nurra arose, her blue eyes glowing, as Elytra pulled back an arrow on her bow.

"Archers, ready!"

The little blue frogs and beetles in the trees took aim at the Dead Kings.

"Fire!"

Their arrows arced across the sky, coming straight at the decayed Kings, hitting them with dusty impact as they collapsed to the ground. The fireflies swarmed the corpses and hovered on top of the Dead, hundreds of them, all bright and beautiful. Out of the swarm flew a familiar erratic lightning bug, who zigged and zagged through the air until he landed on Aniya's shoulder.

"Did you miss me, my love?" Atero cooed into her ear. She smirked and winked at him. Just then, she looked up and saw the butterfly with Athara on his back coming towards them, with Athara waving her arms wildly, trying to get their attention. As they approached the scene, something whizzed through the air and hit the butterfly, causing Athara to fall off. Four of the fireflies zoomed up to catch her and lower her to safety.

Once on the ground she opened her mouth to explain, but then froze up in fear, staring at Aniya. Everyone turned to see Soura standing behind Aniya with a knife pressed against her throat. Cofia screamed for her daughter to stop.

Metwa started towards them, weapon in hand, but was held back by Teok, who glared menacingly at Soura. She returned the glare, looking him dead in the eyes. Her eyes were the same piercing red as the enemies they were facing.

Kaiza laughed gleefully, stepping over the Dead King bodies and making her way closer to Loshi.

"You fools! You cannot defeat me! I have lived a thousand of your worthless insect lives and will live a thousand more. My power is unparalleled. See? Even one of your own understands this. Choose wisely, like she did. Surrender the stone, or she dies."

Loshi looked panic-stricken for the first time in this endless battle. She glanced down at the ring that cradled the precious stone, which still pulsated and glowed brilliantly. This was too great a burden to bear, especially if it meant sacrificing her most loyal companion and friend. She let out a small sigh and began to slide off the ring.

"Stop," a voice commanded loudly.

Standing behind Kaiza was Kaba, holding the body of his dead brother in his arms. He gently set Nrobo down, knelt beside him and looked up at Kaiza with resentment.

"You said you would release them. You said the Mantuu would be freed if they aided you in finding the stone, but they are all dead. You lied to me - to all of us."

He shook his head slowly, sobbing as his tears fell upon his dead brother.

"Kaba - choose your next words wisely," Kaiza replied coolly. Kaba looked at her blankly, and then pulled a poisonous glass ball out from under his cloak and held it up high. Kaiza eyes widened slightly but she kept her composure.

"Kaba," she tried again, soothingly. "Your loyalty will be rewarded. Do not be hardened by this. Had the insects known their place and handed over the stone, our precious Mantuu army would still be alive!"

She moved towards him carefully, evidently aware of what lay in the balance if Kaba could not be quelled. But he did not falter. He shook his head in disbelief.

"You are not in control." his voice now raised. "The stone controls you. Even dead, it has your soul!"

Kaiza's patience was running thin. To her right was Loshi, who now seeing the shift in circumstances, was poised with her sword, ready to fight. To her left was Kaba with the glass ball balanced in his hand. For seconds, which felt like minutes, nobody moved.

Suddenly, Kaiza lunged at Kaba. In one instant, he sidestepped her and looked to Loshi, thrusting the ball up over his head. She raised up her hand on cue and released a green blast of energy, smashing the glass ball and releasing the poisonous liquid all over Kaba and Nrobo's dead body. Kaiza shrieked as the brothers' bodies, dead and alive, burned and fizzled out, turning to dust. The ash scattered in the wind and Kaiza was blinded, not seeing anything around her.

She gazed upon Kaba and her love fizzling to nothing as she let out a heartbreaking cream of sorrow. The ashes scattered in the wind and as they dissipated, Kaiza looked down slowly to see the end of Loshi's sword sticking out of her chest. Slowly starting to burn and smolder. The radiant green light consumed her body as she fell to the ground, her eyes slowly traveling up to meet Loshi's, turning from red, to crimson, to black. Her mouth opened as if to cry out in anger, but no sound came out. Her face slowly began to fade back to what she was once before. She smiled at Loshi with a look of relief and then withered away to a ghastly facade. Her body shriveled, leaving the red stone in her hand.

The red flickered out from Soura's eyes and she stumbled back in confusion, seemingly waking from a trance. Aniya broke Soura's grip and pushed her to the ground before running to embrace Loshi, who cried softly as a wave of relief washed over her. Elytra rushed over to join them, then Teok, then Metwa. All the remaining insects huddled into each other in an act of consolation, joy and sorrow, feeling it strongly and all at once.

* * *

Going back to the village was bittersweet as the casualties were many and only a tenth of the beetles would return. But time would eventually heal wounds, a renewed appreciation and purpose in peace was born, and new beginnings were on the horizon. The Black Forest would remain a memorial for all who perished in what would eventually be known as the Jakiko War. Colorful flowers were planted for all lives lost, even the Mantuu. The Black Forest slowly began to show signs of new life. The grass would become green and the trees would turn rich shades of gold and brown with an abundance of leaves and vibrant blooming flowers.

As for the village, it became somewhat of an epicenter for a mix of many kinds of insects who would go on to live together harmoniously. Aniya and Metwa's souls were united, and they had many many children together; he would go on to become the King's General.

Queen Loshi would make Teok her King, and together they forged a new path in the Forests. One of fairness and love, not just for their own kind, but for all insect-kind. There would be no enforced separation or system based on history, breed or lineage; the only enforcement was one of respect for fellow insects, and the land upon which they all lived. After fighting for the protection of their shared homes in the Forest and the lives of all insects, the tribes of yesteryear seemed to fade away. The lessons and alliances born of that fateful day would echo throughout history, through the ages of ages, until the end of time.

EPILOGUE

"**T**ell us another story Baba!" the antling and beetling children exclaim as Athiok sits back in his chair, resting after finishing the epic tale. He laughs as Loshi enters the hut to begin rounding up the children to return to their huts for bed.

"Now now, it's late and Baba needs to rest."

A little black and green beetle jumps on Athiok's lap and gives him a hug around his neck. "Just one more?"

"Now now, it's far past all your bed times! Tomorrow you will all be waking early for school."

Some of the children sigh begrudgingly but obediently trickle out of the hut, one by one.

Athara walks in shaking her head. "You're going to give them nightmares, Baba." She chuckles softly and begins packing up a satchel. Loshi hands her a blanket.

"Is everything set for the morning?"

"Yes, we will leave at sunrise." Loshi ties up a box tied with twine, then looks at Athiok and smiles warmly. "You are very brave for doing this."

Athiok grins and pats her hand. "It's not only for me, and it's her way of mending old wounds, yes?"

Loshi smiles and gives him a kiss on the forehead. "I will see you in the morning."

In another hut, Teok rough houses with his beetlings as they roll around in the bed. All ten child beetles were black and covered with white spots. When they hear the door begin to open, all of them lay down and pretend to sleep as Loshi stands there with a smile.

"You all must think I was born yesterday, I could hear all of you giggling from 2 huts down!" She shook her head in mock dismay. "Now each and every one of you, go say goodnight to Gama because she is going on a big trip tomorrow, then go straight to bed."

After the children scamper out of the tent, Loshi lays down on the bed and puts her head on Teok's chest. She looks at her hand worriedly.

"What wrong, Loshi?"

"The stone hasn't lit up in over a year. I am grateful, believe me, but maybe I should go with them in case of danger?"

"You can't, Loshi. You are a mother now, the beetlings need you. Plus, they have all the protection they need."

Loshi shakes her head and sighs. "You're right. I just feel a bit uneasy, that's all."

"Everything will be fine. Their journey is short, they will be back by the half moon."

Loshi forces a smile and nods in agreement. She blew out the light, snuggles into their bed and closes her eyes.

* * *

The next day, Elytra and Loshi walk in the morning sun through the flowers of the Black Forest. The memorial site is busy with insects visiting loved ones, planting flowers and paying respects. They meet with Athiok and Athara as they prepare for their journey. Elytra carries her arrows and a bow strapped to her back and Loshi tightens her belt for her.

"Be careful, mother. All of you, be careful. Are you sure you don't need me to join you?"

As she asks this, Soura emerges from a path in the forest and joins the group. She promptly addresses Loshi's concern.

"No need, my Queen. They are in good hands, I promise you."

"Of course, Soura...I trust that they are."

Athara puts the twine-tied box in a satchel and hands it to Elytra, who slings it over her shoulder. Athiok taps his staff on the ground, and smiles at Loshi.

"Tell my grandchildren that there will be another adventure to tell them about when we return."

Athiok and Athara lead the way down to the water to a boat that is waiting. Elytra stops and embraces Loshi tightly. "We will return shortly, and will make sure that the red stone is never found again." She kisses Loshi's head and continues down the path towards the boat.

Soura follows Elytra, and calls back over her shoulder to Loshi.

"Worry not, my Queen."

Unbeknownst to the travelers walking ahead of Elytra, the satchel across her back flashes red for a microsecond, unseen by anyone.

Except Soura. A small smile spreads across her lips as they embark the boat, cast off and sail away into the morning mist.

The End